The Texas Billionaire's Bride

CRYSTAL GREEN

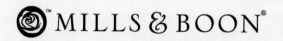

MILLS & BOON®

First published in Great Britain 2010
Large Print edition 2010
Harlequin Mills & Boon Limited,
Eton House, 18-24 Paradise Road,
Richmond, Surrey TW9 1SR

© Harlequin Books SA. 2009

Special thanks and acknowledgment are given
to Crystal Green for her contribution to the
Foleys and the McCords mini-series.

ISBN: 978 0 263 22163 3

CRYSTAL GREEN

lives near Las Vegas, Nevada. She loves to read, overanalyse movies, do yoga and write about her travels and obsessions on her website, www.crystal-green.com. She loves to hear from her readers by e-mail through the "Contact Crystal" feature. There, you can read about her trips on Route 66, as well as visits to Japan and Italy.

To Gail Chasan,
who reigns over these stories
that have provided all of us with
so much life, love and happiness.
Thank you, Gail!

Chapter One

The toughest tycoon in Texas.

That's how Melanie Grandy's prospective employer had been described, to one extent or another, in nearly every article she'd read on the Internet before her quick trip down here.

Thing was, those articles had also painted Zane Foley as a slightly mysterious man who didn't talk about his personal life to the press, even if he led such a public existence otherwise.

But if anyone understood secrets, it was Melanie.

Sitting at one end of a long mahogany table, she watched the head of Foley Industries saunter over the hardwood living room floor of his luxurious Dallas townhouse while he flipped through her personal portfolio, which showed her creative side.

Lordy, it was hard to keep her eyes off of him, although she knew she should.

Yet…

Well, she couldn't help but notice the details. His dark hair was obviously cut at a pricey salon, but in spite of its neatness, some of the ends flipped up ever so slightly near his nape. It made her suspect that he hadn't caught the deviation, and as soon as he did, those ends would be right back in place.

He was also very tall, with broad shoulders stretching a fine white shirt he probably had made to order. His chest was wide, his torso tapering down to a honed waist, his legs long. She didn't know much about his hobbies, but she could imagine him getting fit while horseback riding, could see him sitting tall in a saddle, just as easily as he no doubt commanded a boardroom.

During his scan of her portfolio—he'd seen it during their initial interview two days ago, so was he only perusing it to make her squirm?—Melanie took the opportunity to read between the lines of his silence.

And, boy, did he ever enjoy his silence.

He'd stopped at the other end of the room in front of a stained-glass window, the subdued early May colors bathing him as he glanced over at her. Dark leather furniture surrounded him with a Gothic stillness, each piece angled just so.

Caught checking him out, Melanie's

stomach flip-flopped, but she nonetheless sat straight in her chair, under the intense scan of his hazel eyes.

Probably, it was a bad idea to let her could-be boss know that she'd been assessing him, yet she didn't want him to think she was the type to look away or back down. She was here to get this job, taking care of his six-year-old daughter, Olivia, whom she'd met briefly during the previous interview.

And Melanie was going to win him over, just as his daughter had thoroughly won her at first sight.

Calming her fluttering nerves, she watched as he coolly refocused on her file, as if he'd only glanced her way to take her measure when she'd least expected it.

But was there some satisfaction in his expression?

Had she passed the pop quiz?

"Oklahoma," he said, apropos of nothing. But he'd done it in a low, rich voice that smoothed over her skin just as if he'd bent real close and whispered in her ear.

Melanie made sure her own tone didn't betray that she'd been affected. "I was born and raised just on the outskirts of Tulsa."

They'd covered these basics during their first meeting, and she knew he'd combed through the dossier she'd presented to him, as well. Over these past couple of days, he'd no doubt checked her references, which she knew would speak for themselves. After all, she'd been recommended to him by a business associate he trusted, and that was most likely the only reason she'd gotten her discount-rack shoes in the front door.

Why did she have the feeling that he was going over her information again, just to see if she'd trip up?

Or maybe she was being paranoid. That tended to happen to folks who might have something to hide....

He wasn't saying anything, so she continued talking, supplying more personal details than she had the other day. "It was just me and my mom at first. She put me through day care by keeping the books at a small business, and the minute I was old enough, I dealt with the household after school hours."

Melanie didn't add that those books her mom had kept were located in the back room of the greasy spoon where Leigh Grandy primarily waited on tables between double shifts and numerous dates with the "nice men" she brought home for "sleepovers." In fact, Melanie wasn't even sure which date was her father in the first place; she just knew that he hadn't stuck around.

Now Zane Foley moved toward the long

table where Melanie sat, nearing the other end, which seemed a mile away. It lent enough distance for her to risk another lingering glance at him while he closed her portfolio, placed it on the table, then picked up her dossier.

Darn, he's handsome, she thought before forcing herself to get back into interview mode. But the notion wouldn't go away, brushing through her belly and warming her in areas that should have come with "off-limits" signs.

She would be the nanny, he would be the boss. End of story, if she should be so lucky as to be hired.

"Your information," he said, his gaze still on the papers, "indicates that you started a child-care career early. I'd like to know a little more about your brothers and sisters and how they led to your choice of profession."

"Actually, they were my stepbrothers and stepsisters."

"I stand corrected."

She smiled, avoiding any hardball, but still not standing down.

He didn't smile at all, yet she was getting used to that.

"My mom married the man she called her 'true love' when I was fifteen." It was wonder enough that her mother had finally settled down, but it was even more amazing that her marriage was still intact today. "He had four children. Two of them were much younger than I was—little girls—so I watched over them, in addition to other work. The older two were twin boys, but they weren't around much, because they liked their sports."

Zane Foley cocked a dark eyebrow as he leveled a look at her. "'Were' younger? 'Were' twin boys?"

Melanie tightened her fingers where they were clasped on the table.

He sat in the leather armchair at the other end, perfectly comfortable with being the inquisitor.

Please let me get through this, she thought. She'd spent nearly every last penny in her bank account to get here, traveling to Dallas for these interviews, in the hope that her lucky stars would shine and she'd secure this new job, this new direction.

"You keep using the past tense when you talk about your stepsiblings, Ms. Grandy," Zane Foley said.

"My mistake." She was determined to keep smiling. "We all still keep tabs on each other, even though we're adults." If you counted the odd e-mail as healthy familial relations.

But since she'd left her brood back in Oklahoma, they *were* the past to Melanie. She was the same to them, too, except for her mom, who called quite often for loans.

When her mother remarried, Melanie had ended up in the valley of a no-man's land. Her stepfather had preferred his own kids to her, making no secret about his feelings, either. To him, she was his wife's "bastard issue," and instead of taking out his frustrations about that on Leigh, he'd put it all on Melanie.

Of course, Melanie had approached her mom about this, actually thinking that it would help if Leigh were to address it. Silly her. Her mother had only accused Melanie of trying to sabotage the happiness she'd finally found.

It'd been a stunning moment of betrayal— an instant in which Melanie had realized that her mother would always prefer her guys to her daughter, who'd worked so, so hard to matter more than any of those "nice men."

"When I was a teen," she added, directing the interview back to the more positive aspects of her life, "I took courses at the YMCA for babysitting, and you could say I managed a cottage industry early on. I was booked every weekend, and even during the week, if I could handle it with my studies."

"Evidently, you could, because you aced your classes in school. You graduated with honors, in fact."

"I knew I'd never get anywhere without a good education."

She'd supplied her school records for him, and she was sure someone on his staff had already double-checked those, as well as her employment history.

She only hoped that the one job she'd left off her résumé wouldn't come back to dog her—a gig that had gotten her through college. A paycheck-earner that she preferred to leave behind with the rest of her past.

Her time as a showgirl in what she now considered to be a seedy off-Strip casino in Vegas.

She blew out a breath, continuing, praying she wouldn't give herself away. "Besides babysitting, I took up waiting tables at a burger joint after classes. But I was known as the go-to babysitter of the neighborhood, and that got me more and more jobs. So I gravitated toward that, since I think I was good at it." She laughed a little. "Besides, I could charge more than I made in a restaurant that catered to teens, where the tips were… lacking."

"Industrious," he said, but she couldn't tell if it was just a random comment, or if he was truly impressed.

After all, the Foleys were known far and wide for rolling up their shirtsleeves and working for their fortune. They were self-made men, and Melanie was hoping he would want that in the nanny who was raising his child, too.

"I saved every dollar," she added, "splurging only on my dancing lessons. Lots of them. I couldn't go without."

"We all need an outlet," he said, but he sounded distracted as he looked at the dossier again.

At his next question, she knew they'd entered the most dangerous part of the interview.

"Why did you head toward Vegas right after graduating high school?"

Nerves prickled her skin. "I'd heard the economy was booming at the time, and the opportunity seemed ripe for the taking. The waitress job I got in a local café paid far more in tips than I'd ever made before."

He didn't answer, as if expecting more.

She smiled again, giving as good as she was getting. "Didn't *you* also gravitate there for the same general reason, Mr. Foley? You've developed several projects in the area."

Maybe it was her chutzpah, but a slight grin tilted his mouth.

That was his only answer, and it disappeared before Melanie could be sure she'd even seen it. Then he was right back in boss-man mode, scribbling some notes on the cover of her dossier.

Was he thinking that she was naïve for dropping everything and heading to Vegas, just as thousands of dreamers without his kind of money had done before her? Get rich quick. Double your income with the right gambles.

And gamble she had, just not with money.

She'd been "discovered" one night when

she went out dancing with some fellow students from community college. A talent coordinator from The Grand Illusion casino had given her his business card, inviting her to an audition.

At first, she'd denied him, thinking that her waitress job would hold her. Then her mom had started to write her, asking for loans, and in spite of how Melanie had wanted to escape Oklahoma, she couldn't say no to helping out the family.

And that's when she'd decided to audition. The Grand Illusion had a small, fairly cheesy revue that was half bawdy magic and half sexy musical, although nothing distasteful. Heck, no one even took off their sequined tops. She told herself she probably wouldn't make it anyway. Yet, much to her surprise, she'd breezed through the process, with them offering her a modest wage and, more importantly, the promise of open days during which she could keep going to school and wait a few tables.

It was an ideal setup, and it wasn't as if she was doing any exotic dancing. Just as soon as she had her degree, she'd be done with it anyway.

When she had the degree under her belt, she quit dancing, just as she'd promised herself, and she'd signed on for her first nanny job, thanks to a glowing recommendation from her advisor to his personal friend.

Her employer had been an affluent single mom, a prominent business developer who was in dire need of a helper; and it'd been the perfect job for years, until Melanie's boss got married and decided to become a stay-at-home mother.

And that's how Melanie had come to Dallas at the age of twenty-eight—because her first employer had worked with Zane Foley on the development of a Vegas mega apartment-village complex, and when the business-woman heard that his latest nanny had quit and he needed to hire another one pronto, she'd given him Melanie's name.

He nudged the dossier away from him and, for a heavy moment, Melanie wondered if Zane Foley, a man who seemed to cover every base, had dug deep enough into her life to expose her crowded double-wide-trailer beginnings and dancing days.

Was he going to spring it on her now?

"As you've heard from Andrea Sandoval," he finally said, referring to Melanie's first nanny employer, "I'm eager to get someone in place to care for my daughter. And you almost seem too good to be true, Ms. Grandy, dropping into my lap like this."

She felt heat creeping over her face, mainly because she could just imagine what it might be like to drop into his lap—*Lord have mercy*—yet also because she didn't want to panic at what he might've uncovered.

"No one's perfect, Mr. Foley," she said, hoping he would agree.

He didn't, so she kept talking, seeing if she could maybe use a little flattery as backup.

"Although," she said, "your family seems to come close enough to perfect as it gets."

He remained distant, over on his side of the table. "We're hardly perfect."

"Then you should tell your PR people to stop selling that image," she said lightly. "The media seems to think that the Foleys are the epitome of what's good about our country."

His tone grew taut. "You've been looking into my family, have you?"

How could she deny it? News about the business doings of the Foleys, whose holdings had started from a few oil rigs to an empire based on prime real estate and media interests, was legion. Then there were all their charitable causes, behind-the-scenes political power plays and even the social adventures of Zane's brother, Jason. Hard to ignore, when the media—and the nation—was fascinated with them, even if Zane, himself, tended to avoid the limelight.

"I only did my research," she said, "because I need to make sure you're the right family for me, just as you're making sure I'm right for you."

Her smile returned full force, but not because she was trying to win him over this time. She was remembering the freckled nose and doe eyes of his daughter. There'd only been a short introduction, yet it'd been enough to convince Melanie that she didn't belong anywhere else in this world. Something about Olivia had profoundly tugged at

Melanie, maybe because the girl reminded her of herself—a little lost and isolated.

Zane Foley didn't return her smile. In fact, he seemed intent on avoiding it, while the sun from outside shifted enough to slant a patch of red from the stained glass over the strong angles of his face.

Her chest went tight.

"I like your optimism," he said. "You'd need quite a bit of it with Livie, you know. As I pointed out during our first interview, she's gone through five nannies in six years."

"I remember." Her former employer had already cautioned Melanie. After Olivia's mom had passed away, the girl had rejected everyone she perceived to be taking her mom's place.

Melanie had known from the start that this wouldn't be an easy job; but she wanted to make a difference in the girl's life, because

she sure wished someone had made a difference earlier in her own.

"My daughter's a handful," he said. "I'll
make no bones about that."

"I've got more perseverance than you can
imagine."

"Your predecessors thought they had it, too.
And on their way out the door, most of them
even told me that I ought to think about
applying some of that perseverance I show in
my own business to my household." He
leaned forward in his chair. "Just to give you
fair warning, I don't employ nannies to get
advice from them."

Melanie kept eye contact, thinking that
there was a chink in the steeliness of his
gaze—a darkness that showed more than just
that notorious arrogance.

"Mr. Foley," she said softly, "I'd never
presume to judge *anyone*."

He stared at her a beat longer, then sat back in his chair again, even though he didn't let up with his gaze. It held her, screwed into her, until a slight thrill traveled her veins.

"The family businesses are important to me," he said. "Among other things, they're Livie's legacy, and I intend to give her a great one. As an only child, she'll take over all of my share one day, the oil holdings, as well as real-estate interests."

He said it as if he planned to never get married or have children again. In some weird way, that got to Melanie.

But...jeez. Like she should even be mulling over his most intimate decisions.

"I'm sure your daughter will be grateful for everything you do," she said.

"You should also know that I spend a lot of time defending our investments, not just building them up. That's what takes up the majority of my schedule, and the work's too important for me to spend as much time in Austin with Livie as most people expect."

"Right," she said, figuring she would show him just how much research she'd done. "I read that you have to defend against people like the McCords."

His mouth tightened once more, this time at the name of the family who'd been taking part in a well-known feud with the Foleys for generations.

Oops. She made a mental note never to mention them again.

Zane Foley seemed eager to be rid of the subject. "The bottom line is this—my commitments require a lot of me, and that's why I need someone to depend on for Livie. Someone who's more or less my proxy, enforcing my rules and raising her the way I need her to be raised."

She chafed at his authoritarian tone. What was his daughter to him—another project to develop, like the ones he oversaw in his office?

But Olivia—Livie—was a little girl, and—from what Melanie had seen in her eyes, even for the few minutes they'd conversed—she needed more than rules and routines.

Melanie was on the cusp of saying so when she remembered how much she wanted this job.

"I understand, Mr. Foley," she said instead, keeping the peace, even if she didn't really understand him at all.

He gave her one last look from those striking hazel eyes, and she fortified herself against it—almost successfully, too. He only got her tummy to flip one more time.

Then he rose from his chair, leaving her dossier and portfolio on the table.

Melanie held her breath. Was the interview over?

But he only walked away from the table, toward the hushed hallway.

When he saw that she wasn't following, he waited, and she realized that he wanted her to come, too.

Okay then.

As she stood, she grabbed her suit jacket from the back of her chair, then smoothed down the skirt of the only conservative business outfit she owned.

She made her way across the room to him, her heels clopping on the hard floor, echoing way too loudly for her comfort.

He avoided the door and led her down the hall.

Where was he taking her?

"Livie will receive a full education," he said, beginning to fire off his expectations, "even when she's not in school."

"I'm prepared to teach Livie," she said, excitement churning. He was going to make an offer! "With Ms. Sandoval's daughter, Toni, I planned a different learning experience every day, and doing the same here would be wonderful."

"Livie would benefit from your dance background in particular."

Melanie's blood jolted, but then she realized he was probably talking about all the classes, from ballet to jazz to hip-hop, she'd taken. "Livie has taken dance before?"

"No, but she needs to let out her energy in a constructive manner."

"I see."

"Other than that, her schedule is set. Firm. Don't deviate from it, because she responds well to structure. It might be your biggest saving grace."

Based on Zane Foley's well-ordered townhouse, as well as all his comments, Melanie wondered if, when she arrived in Austin, she would find Livie inhabiting something like a high-class jail.

Fuming inwardly, she told herself to stay quiet. *You want this job, you need this job, so keep your opinions to yourself for now.*

They came to what looked to be a study, with more dark, finely etched antique furniture carefully placed about the room: a desk set that held a laptop computer and organized files, a curio cabinet, shelves teeming with leather-bound books that lent the air a thick, musty scent.

There were also large, framed paintings on the walls, the biggest being an old family portrait of the Foleys that featured brothers Jason and Travis, both of whom couldn't have been more than ten years old at the time, even though Travis looked a little younger. They stood next to their dad, Rex, an affable looking man with a charming grin. Then there was Olivia Marie, their deceased mom, who wore her own gentle smile as she hooked her arm through Rex's.

On the fringes of them all was Zane, who even in his early teens seemed to carry himself with a combination of cockiness and seriousness.

When Melanie glanced away from the portrait, she found that Zane was behind her, standing in front of a different painting. Livie's.

A recent depiction of a sweet little girl in a pink dress, her wavy dark hair held back by a lacy headband. She smiled faintly and held a stuffed lamb.

The picture got to Melanie, yet it was the expression on Zane's face that just about melted her altogether.

Naked love and devotion.

But then it turned into something else—destruction—and Melanie wondered what could have possibly turned one emotion into the other so quickly.

As Zane stared at his daughter's portrait, he wasn't seeing Livie so much as someone else entirely. Danielle.

His wife, dead six years now, but still so agonizingly alive in the face of his daughter.

He couldn't stand the questions that always came afterward: would Livie grow up to be just like her mother? Would his daughter break her own husband's heart someday, too?

Would she have the same mood swings—from dark to manic—that had escalated into that awful day when Danielle had taken her own life?

He glanced away, his attention locking on

the svelte figure of Melanie Grandy. With sunny blond hair that swept her shoulders and blue eyes that seemed to sparkle even when she wasn't smiling, she was the opposite of Danielle and Livie. But from her heart-shaped face to her ill-fitting blue business suit that he supposed she'd purchased just for these interviews—she'd worn the skirt the other day, too—he got the impression of vulnerability. A leggy wisp of a woman, she might not be so different from Danielle after all.

At his inspection, she raised her chin, a habit he'd become familiar with even during their short acquaintance.

No, this woman had a core to her. She also had an innate dignity that sent a buzz of heat through his veins.

Raw beauty, he thought, flashes of an unpolished diamond lighting his mind's eye.

But the glare of it made him realize that

there was no room for any kind of attraction, especially since she seemed to be a perfect fit for Livie. And thank God for Andrea Sandoval's timely reference, because the last nanny had quit, leaving Zane at loose ends. He'd needed a quick hire, and since Ms. Grandy didn't have a criminal record and had come with the highest recommendation from a family friend, he seized the opportunity.

It was just a bonus that his daughter would match well with her new nanny. Livie required someone with spine enough to stand tall and firm, as Ms. Grandy had gracefully done throughout their interviews.

He chanced one last, long second of looking at her, turning the air into a humid fog.

And she seemed to feel it, too. He could've sworn it, because she set her jacket on a nearby end table and folded her hands in front of her while concentrating on the picture, a pink tint to her cheeks.

He got back to business, as well.

Always business. Safer that way.

He moved toward his computer, then woke it out of hibernation mode. He'd brought Ms. Grandy into his study to show her the virtual layout of the Austin estate where Livie resided, but even so, he held off on opening the computer file.

She was still back at Livie's portrait.

"She's a beautiful child," Ms. Grandy said, and he could sense that she was being genuine in the compliment. "I can't wait to start our first day, maybe with some art, where she can express ideas that she might be too shy to say out loud right away."

"The last time a nanny got the paint out she was scrubbing it off Livie for what seemed like hours. It was even supposed to be washable."

He could see a battle playing over Melanie Grandy's face, and it wasn't the first time. She was clearly wondering if she should put in her own two cents about her child-rearing philosophies, instead of listening to his own cynical point of view.

The other nannies had always kept quiet, but when Ms. Grandy spoke, he was pleasantly surprised that she even dared, although it raised his hackles, as well.

"I'm not afraid of some extra cleanup," she said, "if it's the result of something positive for Livie. Maybe she's the type who would benefit from stepping out of that structure she's so used to?"

Now he wasn't even pleasantly surprised with her.

She obviously noticed. "Mr. Foley, I'm not suggesting anything radical. I'm only interested in getting to know Livie."

He didn't tell Ms. Grandy that, aside from that one out-of-control paint day, his daughter generally liked to keep her dresses and hands clean—and it wasn't just at his insistence.

Or was it?

Guilt set in, just as it always did when he thought too hard about how he'd raised—or not raised—his girl. That's why it was better that he'd adopted such a hands-off policy; he was far more adequate at shaping Foley Industries and concentrating on other important matters, like keeping those damned McCords in line.

Plus, he didn't know anything about females at all. That was apparent from what he'd let happen to Danielle.

Melanie was still smiling as she looked at his daughter's portrait, and his heart cracked at how a stranger could so openly display emotion for Livie, when he had such a hard time himself.

He opened the computer file that contained the slides of Tall Oaks.

"Ms. Grandy," he said.

She glanced at him, and he could see the hope in her eyes.

He didn't let that affect him. He and hope had parted company a while ago.

"When can you start?" he asked.

She beamed with one of those warm smiles. "When do you want me, Mr. Foley?"

He couldn't help thinking that, despite the temptation, on a personal level the answer to that would have to be "never."

Chapter Two

After accepting the job and then rushing through a whirlwind of formalities, such as a salary agreement and a computer-aided tour of Zane Foley's Austin estate, Melanie had followed her new employer down the hall and to the foyer, barely able to contain a bubbly grin.

Success!

Melanie Grandy, nanny for the eldest Foley's daughter. She liked the ring of it, and when she found out that she was to be driven in a town car to her motel, where she would pick up her two pitiful suitcases before heading straight to Austin and Livie, she already felt as if she were flying first class.

Okay, maybe *business* class, because it wasn't a limo, but, heck, she'd live.

As they came to a halt near a leather settee under a gilt-veined mirror, she tried not to be too aware of how their image reflected him towering over her. Tried not to get fanciful about how they stood side-by-side, a tense space the only thing separating them.

She fairly hummed from head to toe, as if charged by his presence, but... No. She'd worked hard to get here, and jeopardizing her new position by stepping out of bounds with her new boss had to be the worst idea in all creation.

She tried not to look in the mirror again: his strapping body, his Texas-noble bearing...

"The drive to Tall Oaks is nearly three and a half hours," he said, thankfully interrupting her weakening will to stop lusting after him. "It should give my staff enough time to put together the final paperwork for your hiring and then fax whatever we need to sign."

"I'll look for those papers when I get there then."

"Mrs. Howe might even have the documents in hand when you arrive. She's got run of the house and has been taking care of Livie since the last nanny left less than a week ago."

"I look forward to meeting everyone at Tall Oaks," she said, extending her hand for a deal-closing shake. "Again, thank you. I was really hoping you'd choose me to be a part of Livie's life."

And there it was again—that flash of anguish in his gaze.

But then he took her hand in his, wrapping his long fingers around hers.

Warm, strong…

For a moment she forgot that she was supposed to be shaking his hand. He must've forgotten also, because the hesitation between them lasted a second too long—one in which her heartbeat fell into a suspended throb.

As she pulled in a breath, his eyes darkened back to the cool, detached gaze that had already become so familiar.

But how could she be used to anything about him when she didn't know him at all? she reminded herself, coming to her senses and finally gripping his hand in a professional shake.

She doubted she would ever really know Zane Foley, and that was for the best.

They disengaged, and he stepped away

from her. "I anticipate that you'll be around much longer than the other five."

As he began to walk away, she said, "I sure will."

He paused for a moment, and she thought that maybe he was about to say something else.

But then he moved on, traveling with the ease of a shadow lengthening at sunset, until he blended into the dark of the hallway.

Melanie watched him go, her heartbeat near the surface of her skin.

But she had to get over it; this was her chance to prove that she really was better than the girl who hadn't been expected by her stepdad to do much more than be "bastard issue."

She exhaled, sitting on the leather settee by the door and preparing for the responsibilities ahead of her. Livie—the child who would depend on Melanie to raise her to be all she could be, too.

A stately grandfather clock stood across from her, ticking, tocking, marking the passing seconds as Melanie waited for the driver. Meanwhile, her excitement leveled off to something like a Champagne buzz.

She wondered what the Austin estate would look like in real life, how different it would be from her and her mom's first ramshackle apartment, then the trailer that had served as home back in the day.

On a sigh, she went to grab her suit jacket and purse, preparing for the moment she would walk out this door and into the car, where she would be driven off and away to find out.

Her purse was there, but not her jacket.

She remembered that she'd brought it into Zane Foley's study, putting it down when she'd been looking at the portrait of Livie.

Duh. She'd been too excited by the job offer to pick it back up again.

Okeydokey then. Her new boss had gone in the direction of the study, so she would just scoot back there, knock on the door, grab her jacket, then be out of his hair.

In and out.

But when she went down the hall, her body started doing the jitterbug about seeing him, heart racing, stomping.

Cool it, she told herself. In and out.

She came to the study, noticing that the door was ajar just enough for her to hear his voice. And, Heaven help her, she couldn't resist standing there a second to bask in the appreciation of how he sounded while talking to someone on the phone.

But the more she listened, the more she felt the bass of his voice scratching down her skin, leaving her hair to rise and the heat to play all over her. She thought of what it might be like to see him smile, just once.

Would it feel like a rolling ball of sun inside her stomach? A burning ache that sizzled and made her go weaker than she was even now?

Then he stopped talking, and the person on the other end of the speakerphone started.

The different voice—still appealing, but not nearly as much as Zane Foley's—was enough to kick her right out of fantasyland.

She rolled her eyes at herself, then prepared to knock just before her boss responded to the other person on the phone.

"I hired another nanny today."

Melanie's fist paused in midair.

So help her, she stood rooted there, waiting for what he might say, curiosity killing the cat.

The voice on the other end of the line laughed. "How long's *this* one going to last, Zane?"

He cut him off. "Not amusing, Jason."

Zane's brother, and, according to everything she'd read, the scamp of the three siblings. But he also had the more solid reputation of being the hardworking chief operating officer of Foley Industries—a man who wasn't above getting dirt underneath his fingernails or on his fine suits.

Zane was still talking. "And this time, don't you dare suggest that we bet on her longevity."

"Damn," Jason said, "because if I bet she wouldn't even last a year, just like most of the others, it'd be a smarter proposition than anything Granddad ever put his money on." There was a pause. "So what's this one like? Can you tell me that much?"

In spite of her better judgment, an all-too-human Melanie leaned closer to the door.

Zane was standing by a window with a showcase view of downtown Dallas, across from the gleaming Trinity River. He wasn't sure how to answer his younger brother's question about what he thought of Melanie Grandy.

Should he be honest?

There was something about the new nanny that made him want to tell Jason about her bright hair and brighter smile, even though he knew he wouldn't.

With any luck, he would never see her much, anyway. Staying away from Tall Oaks was best for Livie *and* him.

"This nanny," he finally answered, "enjoys using art to bring out the creativity in children. She likes dance especially, and I think that'll be good for Livie. Ms. Grandy's got a lot of…spirit."

Jason, as perceptive as he was, called Zane out.

"That's not what I meant, and you know it."

"That's all you're gonna get." Zane turned

away from the window and headed toward his desk. It was second in size and comfort only to the one in his downtown Dallas office, where he would be right now if it hadn't been for the interview. "Now, I suspect you didn't call to gab about nannies, Jace. What's on your mind?"

"The McCords."

Zane could almost picture his brother behind his own desk in Houston, as his voice lowered to a more serious tenor. They'd all spent too many years sharing an intense dislike of the other family for Zane not to recognize the signs of a very serious discussion about them coming on.

"Travis gave me a heads up about something I thought you'd want to hear, too," Jason said. "It's about his ranch."

God, the ranch. The property had sparked a feud between the families way back when

Grandpa Gavin had put the West Texas land up for grabs during a poker game that a card cheat named Harry McCord had been manipulating. To add insult to injury, the place had produced silver—the foundation for the McCord jewelry store empire, which catered to the rich and famous and was renowned worldwide as the height of luxury—the premier jewelers of the earth.

"What about the ranch?" Zane asked, an edge to his question. "We signed a long-term lease for the land after the mines were played out. The McCords have no reason to be sniffing around it just yet."

Of course, the McCord matriarch, Eleanor, had once been courted by Zane's father, Rex, so that might've had something to do with the olive branch the other family had offered. And one would think that her generosity would've defused the feud, but her husband, Devon, a devil who was surely getting his just desserts now, after his recent death, had still kept the animosity alive with all his talk about how he'd "won" Eleanor and Rex had lost.

"But," Jason said, "they do seem to be sniffing, and if Grandpa Gavin were still alive, he'd be yelling like thunder. We didn't all pitch in and make that ranch what it is, only so he could live his last years there. Dad accepted the lease because he thought you, me and Travis would benefit from what it could yield."

"Damned straight." Zane would sooner brave the fires of hell, before he saw the McCords relocate Travis, who'd decided to forgo family business in favor of ranching on the property that should've belonged to the Foleys in the first place. "It's just like the McCords to rub salt on a wound. I wouldn't be surprised if they were just trying to remind Travis that they're the ones who still own the property."

"And they've got to know it burns him, with all the blood and sweat he's put into it." Jason's tone grew even angrier. "But I'm not sure it's just about reminding Travis of what's what. The McCord kids are taking after the old man after all."

"Why do you say that?"

"Because, when Devon passed from that heart attack, the clan actually backed off for a while. He was always the one who took the greatest pleasure in the feud. That's what I thought, at least. Now I'm not so sure. Rumor has it that the family lawyers have been taking a real long look at the lease…"

Zane didn't even have to hear the rest.

"…just as if they're trying to find a way to get out of it."

His blood ran hot at the notion of his baby brother losing what meant the most to him.

He wanted to strike out at the McCords, but as his gaze fixed on the portrait of Livie, he pulled his temper back.

Again, he saw Danielle in his daughter.

Living with a bipolar wife had taught Zane that losing his head only made everything worse. Retreating—whether it was into work or into himself—had been the best way to handle her.

She'd also taught him that there was a difference between his personal life and business. In the latter, he could uncork the frustration that built up at home, striking quickly and lethally during deals, allowing him a sorely needed outlet.

And the McCords were just asking for it.

Dragging his gaze away from Livie's image, he refocused on the old family portrait above the fireplace. There was a measure of serenity at seeing the picture that'd been painted just before his mom, his daughter's namesake, had suffered a fatal fall during a horseback ride. His father had tried his best to raise the three boys on his own, but they'd missed their mom terribly.

And sometimes her death even made Zane wonder if all the women in his life would leave before their time.

At any rate, her absence had bonded all of them, and it had molded Zane into a man early on, as he'd taken up where his father had to leave off in raising Jason and Travis. Even now, at the age of thirty-six, Zane felt as if he was still in charge of so much: their holdings, their tanglings with the McCords.

Jason was speaking again: "At first, I wasn't sure why the McCords would be so interested in the ranch right now. I thought maybe they wanted to sell off the acreage, if those rumors about money trouble in their jewelry business are true. But then, what difference would that relatively small cash influx make? Then I thought about the silver mines on the property."

"Those are abandoned, Jace. Tapped out. That's why the McCords leased the land to us."

"I take it that, during this latest nanny search, your ear hasn't been to the ground."

He stiffened until Jason chuckled, revealing that he'd only been injecting a little humor where some was sorely needed. But Zane took his duties as oldest brother seriously. Having the McCords get the best of them during his watch was never going to happen.

"One of my assistants," Jason said, "heard that Blake McCord has been buying up as many loose canary diamonds as possible on the world market."

Diamonds?

Zane started to see where his brother might be going with this.

Jason added, "I imagine you're remembering those news reports from several months ago?"

"The Santa Magdalena Diamond," Zane said. He'd filed the information in the back of his mind, way behind Livie and other more urgent matters, but he sure as hell hadn't forgotten.

A flawless, forty-eight-carat canary gem with perfect clarity, the Santa Magdalena Diamond was legendary, said to transcend even the beauty and brilliance of the Hope Diamond itself. Supposedly, the piece had been mined in India, and was cursed, because it had resulted in bad luck for everyone who ever owned it. It was only when the gem rested with its rightful owner that any personal misfortunes would end.

The diamond had been missing for over a

century, but fairly recently, divers had uncovered a wrecked ship that was supposed to have been carrying the jewel, in addition to other treasures of murky origins.

Really, the only reason the Foleys were interested in the diamond was because their great-grandfather, Elwin Foley, had been on that ship, which might have also been populated by thieves, although that never had been proven. When the transport went down, a few passengers had survived, including Elwin, and according to family stories, he'd snagged the gem, along with a jewel-encrusted chest of coins. But since no one had found either object since, the tale had passed into legend.

However, the ship's recent discovery had resurrected all the rumors, especially since the diamond and the chest hadn't been located.

"The Santa Magdalena Diamond came to

my mind, too," Jason said. "I've been going through a lot of scenarios, but the best I can figure, maybe the McCords believe that Elwin Foley did get away with the gem when he survived the wreck, and he hid the diamond somewhere on the land where Travis's ranch is located now—land that used to belong to Elwin before it passed to Gavin, who lost it in that poker game. And don't you think the Santa Magdalena would pay a few bills for a cash-strapped business?"

"The theory's a stretch," Zane said.

"But the timing's pretty telling. The divers find the shipwreck, rumors recirculate about Elwin taking the diamond, then the McCords express a heightened interest in the property."

"Whatever their intentions, I'm not about to let Travis be hassled by that family."

"Glad you're on board then." His brother sounded as confident as ever.

Zane shot a skeptical glance at the phone. "What exactly did I board, Jace?"

Right about now, his sibling was probably grinning to himself about one of his genius ideas that kept Foley Industries in the black. "If the McCords want to give us trouble, I say we find out about it ahead of time. Cut them off at the pass."

"Your lawyer friends—the ones who got you that information about the McCords looking into the lease—will only get us so far."

"Exactly. I'll be taking matters into my own hands until we know Travis isn't in for some harassment."

Zane waited for it.

"The McCords have a few soft spots," Jason said, elaborating. "One of them is named Penny."

Penny. Penelope McCord. Zane recalled

one of the daughters of the other family—the quiet twin in a set of burnished blond-haired sisters. A jewelry designer who basically kept to herself.

In a contest between her and Jason, the so-called lady killer, she had no chance at all.

"What are you intending, Jace?" Not that Zane had sympathy for any McCord, but…hell, a lady was a lady, and there were limits.

"Nothing fancy. I just discovered we'll be attending the same wedding pretty soon. I've done business with the groom, so he invited me to his big, high-society bash. I figured I might just happen across her table, sit myself down for a rest, offer my own sort of olive branch in polite conversation…"

"…and feel her out for what she might know, without being too obvious about it."

It wasn't a bad idea, and when Jason didn't

say anything, Zane knew he was probably in his desk chair, relaxing with his hands behind his head, content with the plan.

"Okay," Zane added. "A wedding sounds like a good place to casually learn if the McCords have discovered the location of the diamond, and to find out just how true these rumors about the McCords's finances are."

"And if that wedding should turn into something afterward…"

Zane raised an eyebrow. "Jace."

"I'm talking about a coffee date—or whatever."

No, his brother was talking about more than that. Zane knew how Jason loved his women, especially ones as lovely as Penny McCord.

Zane was just about to mention it, when he heard something outside the door.

"Wait a sec," he said to his brother, then went over to check on the noise.

But…nothing.

Still, he thought he smelled a hint of sunshine-like perfume that traced the rough edges of his heart until it felt about ready to fall out of him.

Steadying himself, he closed the door to the dim hallway—and to the very idea of sunshine, too.

Melanie was halfway through the drive to Austin when her nerves finally settled.

She'd only managed to calm down by gazing out the black-tinted window at the passing scenery, as well as chattering with Monty, the town car driver, who, as she now very well knew, had four daughters with tempers as quick as their mama's and tastes way beyond his table wine budget.

The conversation almost made her forget that she'd been standing in a hallway and eavesdropping on her boss. And that her boss had only said that she was… "spirited."

She tried not to let that bother her, but it did. Deep inside, she'd been hoping to hear Zane Foley say that she had a great smile. She'd been wishing for a lyrical description that would've belonged in a song, like maybe there was something in the way she moved….

Right. Anyway, after telling herself that she was being eleven kinds of fool, she'd found that she was sitting there still listening to him and Jason talking about the McCords.

And the Santa Magdalena Diamond.

If Melanie hadn't been confused and intrigued by her new boss before, she sure was now. Since she hadn't been living under a rock, she'd heard about the diamond and how it had been connected to the recent shipwreck discovery. Hearing Zane and Jason discuss all of it just piled one more question upon the other questions that had been weighing in her brain about the Foleys.

Monty glanced in the rearview mirror, checking on her during a lull in their talk. On the downhill side of his thirties, he had thick-lashed, dark eyes that tipped up at the corners in perpetual good humor, dusky skin scraped by a five-o'clock shadow, and a long nose that topped a smile.

"You need me to turn the air on higher?" he asked.

She crossed one leg over the other, aiming her body in his direction and away from the window. "No thank you. It's just…"

"Come on, spill it out to me. Long rides go by a lot quicker with a good discussion."

He was too nice to shut out, but she wasn't going to "spill" anything about Zane Foley.

"I remembered that I left my suit jacket back at the house," she said instead. "Excellent start, don't you think? Mr. Foley probably believes I don't have a brain in me."

Laughing, he shrugged. "Listen, once I fill up my stomach with leftovers from Cook's fridge, I'll be turning this baby right back around, to be on standby for Mr. Foley in Dallas. I'll fetch that jacket for you and make sure you get it soon enough."

"Really? I hate to be such a bother."

He made a dismissive gesture, and she thought it was sincere.

She told him where she left the jacket, before adding, "Must be nice for Mr. Foley to have a driver whenever he needs one. He's worked for it, I know, but what perks, huh?"

He rested his hand on top of the steering wheel. "Mr. Foley doesn't take nearly the advantage of his good fortune as I would. Sure, he has a great place in Austin, but he uses it to house Livie more than anything else. He's never around to enjoy it. And he has that nice town home, too. But with his money? It could've been a castle."

"He *never* comes to Tall Oaks?"

"No. He's not there much at all. Birthdays, Christmas, an annual fundraiser for the Dallas Children's Hospital, and that's about it. Mr. Foley's a busy man, but he gives Livie what she needs otherwise."

Yes, nannies.

Yet, as Melanie had told her boss, she wasn't one to judge, and she needed to keep that in mind.

Monty seemed to have shut himself off from saying any more about it, so Melanie decided to pursue another avenue.

Then she would stop. Really.

"Funny how life works. I mean, if Harry McCord hadn't cheated in that card game with Gavin Foley, the Foleys might've been the ones with the jewelry empire that the McCords developed."

"True," Monty said. "There were five abandoned silver mines on that property. *Five.* That's a lot of cannoli they missed out on because their grandfather made a bad bet." He chuckled. "But, depending on who you talk to outside the family, you're going to get a different story about that poker game."

"What do you mean?"

Monty looked over his shoulder, amusement written on his face, then returned his gaze to the front again. "None of this goes out of the car, understand?"

Heck, she didn't want to summon the wrath of her coworkers by betraying them. "Absolutely."

Her pulse got a bit louder in her ears.

"It's sour grapes, that's what I say. Gavin made the bet, and he should've owned up to it. But it must've been tough to see that land pay off in so much silver to the McCords."

"I can't imagine what it must've been like," she said.

"Fortunately," he added, "the Foleys found their own strike of luck in their East Texas oil fields, but Gavin always claimed that the McCord silver should've been theirs, too. The boys grew up on those sorts of tales, especially young Travis. He practically lived at his grandfather's knee, while our Zane ran the roost over at his dad's house." The driver smiled. "Testosterone Lodge. That's what they called their household after their mother passed on."

Melanie remembered the woman in the family portrait in Zane's study. She'd looked so gentle and caring, traits she'd never really grown up with herself.

"So," she said, feeling an ache in her chest,

"Mr. Foley—Zane—was the second man of the house, right after Rex Foley?"

"Yes, ma'am. And the absence of a woman's guiding touch is why you have the competitive, aggressive Zane Foley, who lords it over the real estate and oil businesses. He's the leader of the pack."

Sitting back in the seat, Melanie allowed the image of Zane Foley's hazel eyes to mist over her thoughts. She sighed without even knowing it, then recovered when she saw Monty watching her in the mirror.

"He's a haunted man, too," the driver said, as if he knew just what kind of effect the boss had on her.

Then again, she wouldn't be surprised if he attracted every woman who came within ten feet of him.

"The missus—Danielle—did a real number on him." Monty shook his head. "You're going to hear about this sooner or later, being a part of the family now, so I'll tell you. But it's not to be talked about to anyone else."

"I understand."

He slumped a little in his seat. "Danielle was bipolar, and during a time when she went off her medication, she took her life."

Melanie instinctively covered her heart with her hand. Now Zane Foley's avoidance of discussing his personal life with the press made sense.

But what had the suicide done to Livie?

To Zane?

She recalled his devastated gaze, and she knew.

"I'm so sorry to hear that," she said softly.

"We were all sorry. It's been almost six years now, but she still has an effect on every moment, every inch of space around us."

Melanie stayed quiet. She was going to live

in what amounted to a haunted house, wasn't she? She was going to walk on the floors where Danielle had walked, brush her fingers along the same walls….

"He married her right out of high school," Monty continued, "but a short time after that, she started showing extreme highs and lows in her mood. Mr. Foley didn't know how to handle that, yet he did everything he could. The doctors even put her on meds, but when she went off of them…"

Melanie closed her eyes, wanting to hear, but not wanting to.

He added, "Mr. Foley isn't a helpless kind of man. He'd always been so good at every-thing—school, home life, sports and then business. But he couldn't come up with any way to aid Danielle, beyond getting her all the professional treatment he could. When she overdosed on pills, he blamed himself and buried himself in work."

She opened her eyes. "How about Livie?"

"She was nothing more than a baby when it happened, but every year she grows to look even more like Danielle. You can imagine what that does to Mr. Foley."

Monty didn't say anything more, but Melanie figured out the rest of it.

Did her new boss fear that history would repeat itself? Was that why he rarely visited Livie, because he thought his daughter would be just like the mother, not only in appearance, but in everything else, too?

Most importantly, had Livie gone through five nannies in six years because she was acting out, missing a dad who found it painful to be around her?

Now the shadows in his gaze made so much sense.

Yet, as the town car purred on toward Austin, all Melanie really knew was that she was on her way to aid a young girl who needed someone to be there, to help her overcome all the anguish.

Even if that someone was a woman who was trying to leave her past behind, too.

Chapter Three

From outside, the Victorian mansion and sweeping lawns of Tall Oaks made it seem as if every single rich-girl fantasy that Melanie had conjured in her life was coming true.

Grand willow and oak trees, majestic wrought iron furniture on the porch under the fine gingerbread woodwork...

But then she stepped foot inside.

As she struggled not to drop either of her suitcases, Mrs. Howe, the estate manager, closed the door behind them, whisking past Melanie on her way to the staircase.

"Ms. Grandy?" the bun-wearing, gray-dressed redhead said, pausing near the faded walnut handrail.

Melanie took a moment to gander at the Spartan foyer, then through the open pocket doors that led to a parlor. The furniture, from a closed rolltop desk set to a loveseat, was what a person would call "bleak." The wooden herringbone floors were bare of warming rugs. And although the ceilings boasted hand-painted images of angels flying in cloudy harmony, the colors were leeched to almost nothing.

Ghostly, Melanie thought again.

Was it too late to quit?

Her gaze fell to a corner of the parlor, where a tall, unpolished gold cage held a lone canary that stirred on its perch, not even singing.

"That's Sassy," Mrs. Howe said. "She's been in the family for a couple of years. Livie likes to try and persuade her to sing sometimes, but that bird doesn't always oblige her. She's a stubborn, quiet little thing."

Melanie wanted to ask how often a canary like Sassy might *want* to warble in a place like this, but instead she blinked herself out of her stupor and followed Mrs. Howe, who was already mounting the steps.

Her suitcases seemed to weigh a ton, made all the heavier by the oppression in here, but she had politely refused Monty's and Mrs. Howe's help outside, and now she was paying for it as she climbed the stairs.

When they arrived at Melanie's bedroom, her expectations were already low. And thank goodness, too, because the bed with its circa 1950 turquoise spread, and the muted lamps resting on the dull chests of drawers, didn't exactly give off any kind of princess vibe.

But she wasn't here to be royalty, she reminded herself.

Still, she recalled what she'd thought back at Zane Foley's townhouse, when she'd wondered if she would find Livie stuck in a high-class jail.

She just hadn't expected to be so right.

Heaving one suitcase, then the other, to the top of the bed, Melanie thanked Mrs. Howe for her welcoming attention.

The manager nodded, continuing the briefing. "Livie's got some playtime at the moment, then it's dinner at six, study time afterward, a bit of relaxing time and bed. She wakes up at seven on the dot for you to prepare her, then drive her to school."

Zane Foley had already gone over all this, even supplying Melanie with directions to the private institution Livie attended for kinder-garten.

"Study time?" Melanie asked, still hung up on that one detail. "Livie's six. What does she have to study?"

Mrs. Howe smiled patiently, and Melanie suddenly saw from up close that the older woman couldn't have been more than forty, given her smooth skin and the absence of deep wrinkles around her eyes. It was the bun and lack of cosmetics that had made Melanie think Mrs. Howe was even more mature at first.

But, beyond that, she couldn't read the manager.

"Mr. Foley," the other woman said, "has Livie read picture books and listen to phonics on her own, applying what she's learned at school."

"So much for being a kid," Melanie said lightly, testing Mrs. Howe, to see just how strict *she* was.

The woman widened her eyes a tad, and Melanie realized that she might have surprised Mrs. Howe with her *spiritedness*.

"Sorry," Melanie said. "It's only that I got the impression Mr. Foley is rather…"

Okay, how could she put this?

Mrs. Howe helped her out. "A hard case?"

Now Melanie smiled.

But the other woman merely adopted a tolerant grin. "He makes sure Livie toes the line, and we all respect that, because he's also a good, fair employer."

The insinuation—Mr. Foley's way or the highway—was clear.

And that was all she said, although Melanie kept thinking, *What about Livie? Is she an employee, too?*

Before she could even dare ask, Mrs. Howe's brown gaze moved to the doorway, focusing on something behind Melanie.

She turned around just in time to see the last of a flowered spring dress flare out of sight in the hallway.

"I believe," whispered Mrs. Howe, "you've drawn some interest."

Melanie's heart folded, as if trying to embrace itself.

Livie.

She walked to the door, but when she got there, no darling little girl was in sight.

Frowning, she glanced back at Mrs. Howe, who was fussing with the bedspread, correcting the wrinkles Melanie had already made by putting her suitcases on the cloth.

Oh, dear.

The manager straightened, ran her hands down her gray skirt. Then she walked out the door, saying one last thing to Melanie as she passed.

"You might want to continue up the staircase, Ms. Grandy, to Livie's playroom." She smiled once more. "Best of luck to you."

And as she eased down the hall, Melanie could've sworn she heard Mrs. Howe add, "A *lot* of luck."

After wondering if her ears were just playing tricks on her, Melanie went to the staircase again, traveling up to a dead end, where a closed door bled light from around its edges.

Lest she doubt that this was Livie's playroom, she saw a sign written in the tremulous letters of a dark purple crayon.

LIVIE.

Somehow, the name felt like a territorial statement, and Melanie hesitated to knock. After all, with the structure put on Livie, didn't she deserve a private place that allowed her some time alone when it was actually scheduled?

After knocking, she waited a moment, listening for a muffled "Come in" that never came.

She put her ear to the wood. Nothing.

"Livie?" she said. "Remember me from the other day? I'm Ms. Grandy, your new nanny. I'd like to say hello to you."

Still no response.

Was the girl even in there?

Cautiously, Melanie tested the doorknob, finding it unlocked. It wasn't a shock, since she doubted that Zane Foley would stand for being shut out of anything.

She thought of her own room in the quiet of night. Her own door creaking open. Mr. Foley paying a surprise visit….

A quiver ran through her, but she chased it away as she pushed at the door.

At first she only saw an austere attic, clean and ordered, with a couple of low, wood tables and several closed chests amongst shelves of toys.

Then, as she looked down, she found herself blocked by an army of stuffed animals that had been hastily tossed in a semi-circle.

A little voice came from the left.

"They don't want you in here."

Melanie glanced toward the sound, finding Livie sitting in a miniature rocking chair, her hands folded in her lap. She was wearing Mary Jane shoes with ankle socks, and her dark hair was held back by a lacy band, the bridge of her nose lightly freckled, just as the portrait in Zane Foley's study had shown.

All that was missing was the stuffed lamb in her hands, but there was something Melanie saw in Livie that the painting hadn't captured sufficiently at all.

The sadness in the girl's big eyes.

It dug into Melanie's chest.

"I thought the room might be empty." She used her smile in a peacemaking fashion, gesturing toward the animals. "You've got a real collection."

The little girl just kept serenely assessing her new nanny, and Melanie thought of how pretty she was, how pretty her mom must've been, too, although she hadn't come across any published pictures of her to know for sure.

Livie glanced at her stuffed menagerie. "Daddy had them sent for my birthday this year. He couldn't visit me this time."

Owie.

Melanie only wished she had a huge bandage that would cover Livie's heart from the damage done to her. She herself knew what it felt like to have a special time like a birthday fall to the wayside. It had happened every year with her own mom, until Leigh would suddenly remember after the fact and try to make it up to Melanie with day-old cake on sale at the bakery.

"So what are the animals doing right now?" she gently asked Livie, even though she knew they'd been set there to bar Melanie from intruding.

The girl stood up from her chair, and the rocker stirred, creaking, adding an odd level of discomfort. She went to a toy shelf, her back to Melanie. "It's their room, and they want you to know that."

And the gauntlet hits the floor, Melanie thought.

"Excellent," she said. "I'm sure you'll agree that there are other ground rules we'll need to establish besides that, Livie. Why don't we sit down to talk about them? I didn't get much of a chance to do that the other day with you, and I'd really like to."

Even with her back to Melanie, it was

obvious that the child was crossing her arms. "My name is Olivia."

"All right." Melanie wasn't going to lose even an iota of patience—not with what this child had gone through with her mother. "Olivia, maybe you'd enjoy lemonade on the back porch with me. How about it?"

"Lemonade has sugar. Sugar makes me hyper. Daddy says so."

Melanie came this close to rolling her eyes, but she refrained. Zane Foley wasn't even here, and he was still being a pain.

"Then if you can't have sugar," Melanie said, "perhaps I can wrangle up some ice tea without sweetener."

Livie sighed, as if exasperated, and went about picking through her toys and ignoring Melanie altogether.

But the new nanny didn't go anywhere. Nope. She just stood there and memorized the details of the room, the display of toys that would tell her something about Livie, whether or not the child wanted her to know.

Stuffed animals—dogs, sheep, dolphins. All gentle creatures.

Puzzle boxes nearer to the doorway that looked to have never even been opened.

Dolls—especially Barbies.

Melanie grinned to herself, then retreated down the stairs, but only because she had a secret weapon that had also served to disarm her first charge in those initial days with her.

She went to her room, to one of the suitcases, and pulled out a smaller bag that was filled with sewing materials and doll dresses. She'd taken up this hobby early, back in her babysitting days, because she'd found that Barbie clothes were catnip for ninety-nine percent of all little girls.

Then she went back to Livie's domain.

There, she sat within the semicircle of sentinel animals and took out the most exquisite wee bridal dress. She began to fluff the airy sleeves and spread the sheer, belled skirt.

She didn't call attention to herself, but then again, she didn't have to.

Over the course of the next few minutes, Livie gravitated from one shelf to the other, closer to Melanie, although she wasn't obvious about it.

Melanie lay the bride's frock on her knee, smoothed it out, then reached into her bag for a long, splashy pink satin party dress that always made Barbie look like even more of a knock-out.

As she traced a finger over its sleekness, the glitz took her back to neon and jangling slot machines, and she shoved the memory of her old casino life away, just as if it were baggage she would keep in her own attic.

Soon, Livie was near Melanie, although still on the other side of the animals. Melanie glanced up, as if surprised to see her.

She casually offered the wedding dress, and Livie touched it with her fingers, then drew them away.

"It's okay," Melanie said. "Why don't you get one of your dolls and see how she looks in it?"

Without meeting Melanie's gaze, Livie went across the room to her toy shelf, and when she returned with a brunette Barbie, her gaze was fixed on that dress, her eyes shining.

As she put the frock on her doll, Melanie's gaze lit on the bridal dress, too, unable to look away, as thoughts of Zane Foley taunted her with something she knew she would never have with a man like him.

Zane hadn't moved an inch from his desk, ever since getting off the phone with his brother. Jason and he had been cut short by a slew of phone calls from Zane's office, and he was just wrapping up the latest one while he multitasked, paging through a bound hard-copy file for the Santa Magdalena Diamond that he'd pulled from his library.

Magazine articles, news transcripts—everything, he thought, as he scanned a computer printout about Great Grandfather Elwin and his alleged role in making off with the gem. Zane was going through it all, just to see if he could find something he'd missed, a clue that might let him know where that diamond could've gone—something to lead him to it before the McCords saw it first.

Meanwhile, he listened to his assistant, Cindy, as she talked over the speakerphone.

"Just in case you're wondering," she drawled in her wry manner, "we've got your

Fourth of July Dallas Children's Hospital charity event about set and ready."

"Two months ahead of time?"

"I aim to please, sir. Expect a crew to be descending on Tall Oaks within the month, to start whipping the estate into shape. You've commented yourself that it's not exactly in showcase form."

Zane was still looking at the diamond file. Sometimes Cindy could be incredibly direct, like a less-tactful version of—

As he thought of Melanie Grandy, his gaze drifted from the paperwork. Lively blue eyes, a spark in every gesture…

He wondered how she was getting on with Livie so far. Wondered if he would be having to hire another nanny soon.

Something like disappointment sank within him, but he ignored it.

"Next item on your list?" he asked.

"I'm working on your other charity commitments, but there're no updates on those yet. However, we've got a lot to cover about that state representative seat. Judge Duarte's been ringing my phone off the hook to get through to you about running during the next election."

"I know." Zane had been avoiding any and all calls about it. "That man's head is thicker than timber. What's it going to take to get him to understand that I'm not interested in running for anything?"

"You'd be perfect for it, Mr. Foley. Besides, your family isn't exactly the hands-off type when it comes to politics."

True, but Zane preferred to let his fundraising abilities and civic activism do the talking.

"I'll call Duarte tomorrow," he said. "By the way, isn't it about time you headed home? Mike probably has dinner all cooked up for you."

"Carne asada. I love being a newlywed and having a barbecue master for a hubby."

"Then scram before he leaves you."

"Yes, sir."

With that, they ended the call, but it wasn't two minutes later that Zane got another one.

He didn't mind, though. Business kept him going, gave him less time to think about everything else.

He saw his youngest brother Travis's number on the caller ID, so he donned his earpiece, left the study and went to the kitchen, since his stomach felt empty.

"Hey, Trav," Zane said as he walked down the dark hall. He knew every unlit step by heart. "You out on the range?"

"Just got back in from seeing to some fences that needed fixing. I hear Jason told you about the McCords' unwelcome interest in the ranch."

"That's right."

"I already talked to him about the grand plan with Penny McCord. I don't love this sneaking around Jason's going to be doing with her," he said, "but if it clears the air in any way, I'll live with it."

He distrusted the McCords just the same as any of them, yet Travis was a cowboy, a loner, and loathed being distracted by what he thought to be less important matters, such as the other family's "sniffing around."

"Jace and I didn't want to go forward on anything without your knowing it," Zane said, opening the fridge, discovering that it didn't contain much more than a drop of milk in a carton, and several long-neck bottles of beer. He grabbed one of those and headed for a pantry cupboard.

"Jason said the same thing." Travis waited a beat, and Zane could hear the change in his voice as he switched gears. The less time he could dwell on the McCords, the better. "Aside from the drama, I hear you've got yourself a new nanny. Jason thinks you like her."

Zane almost dropped his beer, and it wasn't just because Travis was being a smart-ass.

It was because a bolt of contained need had shot through him, released from somewhere deep down, where he'd repressed the longing, thinking that it was useless.

He recovered in time to say, "For Pete's sake, do you two live in a middle-school locker room?"

Travis laughed softly. "Just bustin' your chops. But he did tell me that Livie's finally going to have some dedicated company again. I have to say I'm glad for that, because I imagine she's lonely over there."

Zane wrapped up all remainders of desire that he'd felt this afternoon, packing it tightly away at the mention of his daughter.

Travis and Jason adored their niece, and occasionally they tried to let Zane know that he could improve his fatherly skills.

But they didn't understand how tough it was. They hadn't lived with Danielle, hadn't tried to keep it all together after her death.

How could they understand Zane's failures and his need to keep it from happening again with Livie?

"Zane," Travis said, clearly knowing that he was treading on thin ice, "I know the anniversary of Danielle's death is coming up, and I'm sorry for broaching this again, but what're you going to do about Livie?"

"Stay out of this, Travis."

Every inch a Foley, his sibling did no such thing.

"You think it's a good idea to keep sweeping every mention of Danielle under the carpet?" his brother asked. "It's not like Livie's ever going to forget she had a mother. Your pre-tending as if Danielle never existed is only going to do more harm than good."

Zane's temper crept up, squeezing his temples.

But maybe *"temper"* was the wrong word. *"Remorse"* was more like it.

"I don't need to hear this from you," he said.

"Zane—"

Unable to stand any more, he hung up on his brother and leaned against the cupboard in the darkness of his home, wanting to say he was sorry.

And not just to Travis, either.

At ten minutes to six, a bell clanged from downstairs, and Livie jumped up from her spot on the floor in her upstairs playroom, immediately beginning to tidy all the Barbies and stuffed animals she'd brought out.

"Dinnertime," the little girl said, as serious as ever.

Melanie gathered the doll clothes, watching her charge bustle here and there, as if her life depended upon a spic-and-span performance. Once again, she felt for Livie, who'd actually began removing those stuffed animals bit by bit, until she'd opened a hole for herself to come through and get closer to Melanie.

Of course, she'd done it slyly, as if her new nanny wouldn't notice, and Melanie had played along, trying not to look too happy about even that bit of progress.

Livie was so efficient that she had most of the stuffed toys back in place before Melanie had cleaned her own mess, and before she knew it, the little girl was standing at the side of the door, her back straight as she expectantly folded her hands in front of her.

Melanie wasn't sure what was happening

until Livie said, "This is where you're allowed to come in to make sure everything is in its place."

Oh. Right.

But Melanie kept near the doorway, on her side of the invisible semicircle that the girl had created earlier with the stuffed animals. "Do you mind if I come in, Olivia?"

The child gave Melanie a sidelong glance, as if she couldn't believe what she was hearing.

The hint of a smile pulled at the corners of her mouth, revealing darling dimples, and she nodded. And went back to not smiling.

Melanie didn't mind, though; she entered the room, making sure all the dolls they'd played with were lined up on the shelves. She was tempted to mess them up ever so slightly, just because she wondered what Zane Foley would do if he saw the aberration, yet she resisted.

"Top-notch job," she said, turning around just in time to see Livie watching her, then quickly fix her gaze on a spot above Melanie's head. "You're a hard worker, aren't you?"

"Yes, Ms. Grandy."

She walked toward her charge, wishing she could rest her hand on Livie's dark head or touch her shoulder, offering some reassurance.

But sensing that this wouldn't go over well—not just yet—she instead said, "Let's get washed up and see what's on the menu."

Livie spent one more second checking Melanie out, then spun around and dashed down the stairway.

"Careful," Melanie said, and the girl stopped, then slowed down, using the banister.

But, as if realizing that she was being too nice to the nanny she still had to haze, she sped up again, yet not enough to be chastised for it.

Good heavens, Melanie thought, wishing she had a million more Barbie clothes to use as placating lures from this point on.

After cleaning up herself, she went to the dining room, which was just as stark as the rest of the house, with a long table—an item Zane Foley seemed to favor for the distance it established between diners—and plain chairs and a sideboard. The only ornamentation, if you could call it that, was a bland chandelier, with frosted glass cups lending illumination.

Livie took a seat at the long side of the table, and just as Melanie sat down opposite her, Mrs. Howe appeared through a door.

It was only when the manager cleared her throat that Melanie noticed Livie's saucered eyes that stared at her new nanny sitting at the main table.

Oh.

"Ms. Grandy," Mrs. Howe said, "Livie will eat here. Why don't you follow me?"

Livie looked down at her table setting, and Melanie couldn't read her expression.

Without causing a scene, Melanie rose, went through the door with Mrs. Howe, but stopped the manager before they got too far.

"I appreciate that there are certain ways you've done things around here," Melanie said, "but I'd really like to be with Olivia tonight. She's not resisting me as much as she did earlier, and if I could continue that streak…"

Mrs. Howe's face was unreadable. "That would be between Mr. Foley and you, Ms. Grandy. He's the one who wants the help to eat in the kitchen."

Really now?

"Well, I'm willing to answer to him for

this," Melanie said evenly, smiling at the manager.

With a curious look, the woman left her alone.

Truly alone, too, because when it would come time to answer to Zane Foley, it'd be all on Melanie.

But, seriously—like she was going to leave poor Livie to eat by herself?

She went back into the dining room, and when the girl looked up, her sad eyes softened a tad.

Then she glanced back at her plate; but it was too late—because she'd already wrapped her tiny fingers around Melanie's heart.

She waited, not trusting herself to speak for a moment.

Finally, when she'd gotten some composure, she said, "I like it better out here. It's nice and quiet."

"Yes." The girl peeked at Melanie.

Melanie gave her a reassuring grin, and from the way Livie held back her own smile, she guessed that the child understood that her nanny had risked a spot of trouble just to eat with her.

The door behind them opened again, and a young blond man with a scraggly beard stepped through with a table setting for Melanie. He was dressed in chef's whites, so she assumed he was the cook.

Without saying anything, he nodded to her, then winked.

Approval. Thank goodness there was *someone* here who wasn't giving her the near-silent treatment.

Then he left, but only to bring out a well-balanced meal of meatloaf with broccoli, fruit cocktail and macaroni and cheese.

Livie dug right in after the cook was gone, then slowed down when she saw Melanie's are-we-at-the-zoo? expression.

She swallowed. "I'm only eating fast because Mrs. Howe said I can play with my new present from Daddy after dinner and study time."

"Oh?"

The girl nodded, a fork full of mac and cheese halfway to her mouth now. "An American Girl doll. Daddy sends one every week if I'm good."

Livie chowed down again, but Melanie didn't touch her food yet. Her stomach roiled a bit at the thought of how Zane Foley couldn't be bothered to visit his daughter, seemingly buying her off with gifts instead.

And when Livie next spoke, she only confirmed Melanie's heartsick suspicions.

"I like the dolls," she said softly, "but they'd be even better if *he'd* bring them to me."

Melanie held back a swell of emotion. This little girl needed the love and attention of the only parent she had left.

Why couldn't he see that?

"I know what you mean, Olivia," Melanie said, thinking of her own mom. "I know exactly what you mean."

The child didn't look up from her plate, but her next words revealed everything, even if her tone was just as subtly guarded as it'd been earlier in the attic.

"My name's Livie."

Melanie swallowed back the tightness in her throat, then picked up her fork so they could eat their meal together.

She only wished that Zane Foley could be here, too—for his daughter, of course.

But when an unwelcome, low burn heated her belly, pooling down and down, Melanie admitted that maybe she also wanted him here for a different reason altogether.

Chapter Four

The days sped by with more dolls being delivered to Livie, more meals that Melanie took at the table with her charge and even more instructional hours for the girl.

But to supplement those regular study sessions, Melanie also brought her love of dance into the playroom, where Livie had been allowing her nanny to slowly but surely spend more time.

Still, out of all of those passing days, Zane

Foley hadn't paid a visit to Tall Oaks once, nor sent for Livie to come to Dallas.

Not even one darn time.

Oh, sure, there'd been phone calls to the little girl—about one every few days—but Melanie guessed they were more out of habit than a true need to connect with Livie, because each one left the child looking sadder than ever.

Yet, this only encouraged Melanie to step up her "save Livie" campaign, paying the child as much attention as the girl was open to on any given day. She showed her that someone really did care, even if Livie turned away from Melanie at times, and let those stuffed animals that had protected the playroom on that first day speak for her.

"They want you to leave them alone," Livie would say sometimes. "They don't need anyone to pretend they like them."

Little did she know that Melanie wasn't pre-tending; so the newest nanny hung in there, doing her best to give Livie her all.

She just wished she knew how to confront the problem of Zane Foley himself. How to talk some sense into him. How to make him see that he wasn't doing Livie any favors by staying away.

Melanie wanted to despise him, but then night would come, when the wind thumped branches against the old house, when the moon shined through her window and lulled her to close her eyes and imagine how it had felt to touch him when she shook his hand.

How the contact had shaken her to the core.

And morning would arrive again, and she'd go right back to thinking about what to do about him and Livie.

Today, as the June sun spilled through the attic window, Livie had decided to celebrate summer—and her leaving kindergarten behind—with an impromptu performance for some of the house staff. Accordingly, the audience of two sat on the quilts spread over the floor in front of a makeshift blanket curtain that Livie and Melanie had constructed.

The little girl was behind it now, while Mrs. Howe and Cook waited.

Cook, who was in his chef's whites, crossed his legs Indian-style and grinned at Melanie, who was just in front of the curtain, ready to open it. His name was Scott, and from that first week forward, he'd encouraged Melanie to call him that.

Meanwhile, Mrs. Howe sat in a ladylike position, her knees to the side, her pale skirt covering her legs. Her name was Sue, but when Melanie had dared use it one time, she'd gotten a raised eyebrow and hadn't tried it since.

"Is it almost showtime?" Melanie asked Livie.

"Five minutes!" the girl said from behind the curtain.

"Okay." Melanie smiled at the audience, then walked toward them, sitting on the edge of the quilt while making sure her sundress skirt was in place. "Last-minute rehearsals behind that curtain, I imagine," she whispered. "Livie's nervous."

Scott shrugged, but he was so mellow that Melanie often suspected life was one big "oh, well" for him, anyway.

"It's her first show," he said. "The squirt can take her time to give us the premiere."

Mrs. Howe sighed at the nickname "squirt." She sighed a lot about Cook's surfer-in-Texas attitude.

Melanie grinned at Scott. "I guess that's the beauty of summer—no school to work a schedule around."

"But," Mrs. Howe said, "a schedule's still important."

During the past weeks, Melanie and the manager had experienced some…philosophical differences…about many things, although Mrs. Howe hadn't tipped off Zane Foley to the new nanny's slight adjustments. At least, that's what Melanie suspected, because her boss hadn't rung her up yet to give her a talking to or fire her.

"You're right," Melanie said, "schedule's are important, and we still have one. Livie does well with them, so it seemed counterproductive to change her way of life midstream. But there's room for flexibility when it's warranted."

Scott playfully made the sign of the cross, like he was extending Mrs. Howe some help in fighting off Melanie's words.

"Mrs. Howe," he said, "would lose her mind

without lists and charts and diagrams. Them's fightin' words, Mel."

The manager made a dismissive gesture at him, as if that would cause him to disappear, but she had an air of barely restrained amusement just the same. Melanie had decided that Scott was like Mrs. Howe's little brother, and their relationship was one long drive in a backseat where they get on each other's nerves.

Nothing romantic, though, Melanie thought. Mrs. Howe had a husband down the hill in their own cottage, and Scott had mentioned something to Melanie once about a serious girlfriend.

Livie's voice came from behind the curtain. "Almost ready!"

"Okay," all the adults answered back.

Scott kept looking toward the performance area, but now there was something pensive about him.

Melanie leaned near so her voice wouldn't have to carry. "What is it?"

He started to talk, then stopped, shrugged and smiled vaguely.

Melanie knew if she waited long enough he would go on.

And he did.

"It's nice to see her like this," he said. "I don't know exactly what you're doing, Mel, but I can't imagine Livie ever wanting to give any kind of performance before you came along."

Melanie blushed, knowing she was no miracle-worker.

Whispering, she said, "Livie's giving her performance in an attic, so it's not as if this is some grand coming out for her."

"Oh," Mrs. Howe said, "but it is."

For the first time, Melanie saw a pleased openness about the other woman, and that took her aback.

Melanie glanced away from the others and their approval; she wasn't willing to accept credit for anything, because there was still such a long way to go. There were even times when Livie would sit quietly staring out the window, and Melanie feared that no one would ever be able to get in. And there were the days when Livie could be so stubborn that it stretched Melanie's supply of patience to the breaking point.

Those were the moments when she could see why the other nannies had walked away. However, Melanie had come to the realization that it hadn't been Livie who'd driven the others away, so much as it'd been the hopelessness of the situation itself. Maybe it even broke their hearts to be so strict with the child.

The difference was that Melanie vowed to never give up.

"At any rate," Scott said, getting her attention again, "you're a real find, Mel. Mrs. H. agrees with me, too."

The manager hmphed. "I wasn't sure at first."

"You came around quick enough from the opinion you used to have." Scott made his voice higher, imitating Mrs. Howe. "'Mr. Foley has no idea how to pick 'em, does he? Set a pretty face in front of him, and he's sold.'"

"Cook," Mrs. Howe admonished.

"That's what you said," Scott added, that little-brother mischief in his eyes.

But Melanie was barely paying mind to that.

Pretty?

Zane Foley had only called her "spirited" on the phone to his brother, but did the employees at Tall Oaks know something else?

And... *Wait.*

Had the *other* nannies caught Zane Foley's eye?

A spear of jealousy stabbed her, and she scolded herself. Ridiculous to even be thinking it. Or to believe he'd hired her because she was slightly above average.

Still, she'd been spending so much time tuning in to any and all clues from the staff about the distant Mr. Foley that she all but vibrated now with this tidbit from Scott. No one but Monty had really talked about their boss—or the subject of Danielle—so she was much too open to any leaked detail.

"Ready!" Livie finally called out.

Melanie stood and went to the boom box by the curtain. She selected the Enya song Livie wanted to dance to and pulled back the material to reveal the little girl, who was dressed in a pink leotard and ballet slippers that Zane Foley had sent the second day of Melanie's tenure.

Mrs. Howe and Scott applauded, but as the synthesized strings began to play, the child just stood there, staring at them.

"Livie?" Melanie stage-whispered.

The child fixed her doe eyes on her nanny, as if forgetting everything Melanie had taught her about any of the dances they'd tried so far. They hadn't even come up with a routine for this performance, because Melanie had just encouraged her to do whatever the song inspired at any given moment, whether it was ballet or contemporary or even a few tap moves.

Maybe that had been a mistake.

Maybe Livie *did* need that firmer structure she was so used to. Maybe she couldn't depend on anything else.

Heart contracting, Melanie took the girl's hands and began to dance with her. Livie reacted immediately, still looking into her nanny's eyes as if nothing else existed, and laughing as she imitated everything Melanie did.

Soon the song was over and the audience clapped again, shouting out their "bravos" as the performers took their curtsies.

Livie's cheeks were flushed while she kept smiling up at Melanie.

The breath caught in Melanie's throat. No one had ever looked at her that way—not even the other children she'd cared for—and without thinking, she bent to wrap her arms around Livie.

The girl hugged her back, resting her head on her nanny's shoulder.

For a moment the world seemed to stop, to clarify everything about what Melanie wanted: being needed and being able to give as much as she got from just one simple embrace.

Her imagination kicked into motion, picturing another pair of arms around them, hugging them all close together, creating the cocoon of a family that Melanie had never truly had.

Zane Foley's arms.

The sound of hammers against the back of the house knocked Melanie out of the moment. It was the maintenance crew, getting Tall Oaks in shape for the charity event that would take place here on the Fourth of July. Obviously, their break was over.

At least Livie would get to see her father then, Melanie thought, drawing back from the girl and smoothing a dark, wavy strand of hair away from her face.

As if she could read Melanie all too well, Livie got that sad look in her eyes, then hugged her nanny once more before backing away and going to Mrs. Howe and Scott, who congratulated her with their warm gestures.

It was nice while it lasted, Melanie

thought. Maybe *she* was just as starved for affection as Livie.

When Mrs. Howe's phone rang with a chirping tone, Livie listened to Scott as he told her about his favorite part of the dance. In the meantime, the woman extracted the device from her pocket, checking the ID screen, and her relaxed demeanor altered as she answered the phone.

"Good afternoon, Mr. Foley," she said.

A burst of adrenaline jolted Melanie from head to toe, warming her—no, *heating* her—through and through.

She shut off the boom box, lending the attic silence as she noticed that Livie had gone bright-eyed and hopeful, watching Mrs. Howe talk to her dad.

Once again, Melanie hurt for her, because she knew that he'd just called Livie yesterday and he wasn't yet scheduled to do so again.

Darn it all, what could she *do* to take care of this situation?

Mrs. Howe kept talking to him, nodding, assuring him that the maintenance crew was making headway with the exterior of the mansion. In the meantime, Livie grabbed the manager's skirt, as if to get her dad's attention through Mrs. Howe.

Unable to stand it anymore, Melanie went to Livie, resting a hand on the girl's head.

"Can I talk to him?" the little girl whispered to Mrs. Howe.

Something like a heartfelt reaction overtook the manager's face. She looked at Melanie almost regretfully, while tacitly asking her to usher Livie out of the room so Zane Foley could conduct business without interruption.

Anger boiled in Melanie, taking over—or maybe even mixing—with the surge of awareness she'd been feeling before.

She got down to Livie's height. "Maybe we should try calling him later," she whispered, "after business hours?"

That sorrow—so familiar, so gut-wrenching—consumed Livie's gaze.

Scott shook his head while wandering out of the room, and Melanie thought that he might've been expecting more of her—the woman who'd taken Livie under her wing.

And shouldn't he?

Mrs. Howe signed off, silent, as if not knowing how to react or what to say to the little girl who'd been all but forgotten here at Tall Oaks.

Forgotten. Melanie knew exactly what that felt like—to live in a place where there were people crowded all around you, but you didn't seem to exist in any significant way.

It was the last straw.

"Know what?" she said, tweaking Livie

under the chin, trying to distract her, even though it was so tough, with her throat choking every word.

Livie's mouth formed around a silent "What?" She was trying hard not to cry.

"I'm going to make sure you see your daddy soon," Melanie said, skimming her fingers over the girl's hair.

She heard Mrs. Howe gasp but ignored it, because Livie's eyes had already gotten that gleam of hope in them, and Melanie would move mountains to make her promise come true.

Too late, she wondered if she was crossing a line—if this vow would get her fired. Flying in the face of Zane Foley's wishes might take away all the security she'd won by landing this job.

But no one had been fighting for Livie.

"Really, Ms. Grandy?" the little girl asked,

as if she couldn't believe any promises when it came to her dad.

"Really." Melanie stood, facing Mrs. Howe. "Father's Day is just around the corner, isn't it?"

She wasn't so used to celebrating the holiday, but she knew it was sometime near mid-June.

"Ms. Grandy…" the manager began in a warning tone.

Brushing that aside, Melanie took Livie's hand and squeezed it. "We're going to make a present for him. And we're going to be hand-delivering it."

As Mrs. Howe closed her eyes and sighed, Melanie smiled down at her charge, who was already hopping up and down.

"Yay!" Livie danced in front of a cautious Mrs. Howe. "We're going to Dallas!"

Yes, they were going to Dallas.

And somewhere in the back of Melanie's mind, she realized that perhaps the trip was just as much for *her* to see Zane Foley as it was for Livie.

Even if it was a Saturday, it'd been a typically long day at the office for Zane: putting the finishing touches on acquiring an old, junky amusement park near San Antonio, with the intention of polishing it into a environmentally conscious spa complex; having yet another needless discussion with Judge Duarte about that state representative seat; hearing from Jason about how he'd met Penny McCord at that wedding this past weekend.

Zane showered and donned some sweats and a T-shirt. All the while he went over what his brother had told him about pouring the charm on Penny, as he'd tried to subtly coax any information he could about her family's interest in Travis's ranch. She hadn't seemed to know much, and Jason hadn't believed it, so he'd decided to pursue her further, perhaps through another "chance" meeting soon.

Truthfully, it'd all worn Zane out—maybe because, in spite of his support of the plan, it still wasn't sitting well with him.

Then again, this had to do with the McCords, so all was fair.

Since he'd already had dinner at his downtown desk, he grabbed some paperwork about the Santa Magdalena shipwreck from his briefcase, then went to the living room and turned on the TV, thinking he would sit and read for a spell.

But he was interrupted by a knock on the door.

Zane looked at the clock on his DVR unit. 8:00 p.m.

Who the hell was paying a visit?

He set down the papers and went to the foyer, accessing the security video screen console that was hidden in a wall panel.

When he saw a hint of blond hair, his libido instinctively went wild because he'd been imagining that same light shade, plus a slender body and long legs, every night since he'd met Melanie Grandy.

And as his vision focused, allowing him to see the rest of her standing right there, in the flesh, in front of his door, the air deserted his lungs, stirring him up, electrifying him in a way he hadn't felt for years.

He hadn't had time for it, and business took up all his energies. Women had gotten him into too much trouble before, and staying away from them made life easier.

Didn't it?

Angered at all the questions—and even more so at Melanie Grandy's presence—he was about to press the security speaker and demand to know what she was doing here.

Then he spied Livie next to her nanny, holding Melanie Grandy's hand, and paused.

Livie.

Guilt consumed him until he banished it, focusing instead on the anger because it was so much simpler to understand.

He unlocked the door, yanked it open, and the force of the motion made the warm air outside stir Melanie Grandy's hair.

The soft-as-silk strands that he'd been fantasizing about…

"Hello," she said as calmly as you please, with a polite smile to match.

But Livie's grin was much more excited as she said, "Hi, Daddy!" and held up a light blue construction-paper card decorated with feathers and sequins and doodads.

It read "Happy Father's Day!"

The sight almost brought him to his knees, and that made him even angrier.

Still, he gently took the card from Livie, giving her all he could with a half smile that he hoped expressed everything he wasn't able to say out loud, because he knew emotions and investment in them would only backfire someday.

When he didn't say anything else, Livie's smile faltered.

Dammit. Dammit to hell.

But he didn't know how else to handle her.

The helplessness got to him again, and he refocused his frustration on a less vulnerable target.

The nanny.

"I don't remember arranging a trip out here," he said, his teeth clenched because he was trying so hard to rein in his temper.

And his inadequacy as a father.

She didn't back down even an inch.

"Father's Day is tomorrow, and we thought we'd wish you a happy one. Livie made you a gift, too."

He could see the nanny squeeze his daughter's hand, urging Livie to present a slim box to him. But the child seemed reluctant to do so after how he'd responded to her card.

He couldn't blame her.

Unable to stand himself, he relented just this once and bent down to Livie, accepting the box, then opening it to find a hand-sewn tie made out of flannel R2-D2 material.

Livie spoke up quietly. "Ms. Grandy helped me."

"It's made out of pajamas she'd grown out of," the nanny said.

God help him. He just stared at the gift, thinking he'd never seen anything so wonderful in his life.

But when he glanced at his daughter, he saw Danielle's smile—the sweet, innocent expression his own wife had worn when they were young.

Back then, it had been so easy to think everything was going to be okay. Yet, then hell had hit, and he'd realized that he should've been so much more careful.

He tried to say something to Livie, failed, then tried again, even though the words scraped on the way out.

"Thank you, sweetheart," he finally managed, touching her cheek.

"You're welcome."

He could see in her eyes that she wanted more than just a thank you, so he awkwardly held open his arms.

She hesitated, but Melanie Grandy helped out by guiding Livie forward.

When his daughter fell against him, he

closed his eyes, squeezing her tight. Probably too tight, because she backed away and went back to holding her nanny's hand.

His own daughter, preferring a near stranger.

But that's what *he* was, wasn't he?

If thoughts could make a person bleed, he'd be dying.

"Why don't you go inside, Livie?" he said, his tone measured. "The TV's on."

"TV?" she asked, clearly intrigued about an activity she rarely got to indulge in.

He gestured for her to enter, and after she did, he tried to contain himself in front of his guest.

But there was too much to bottle up: the frustration, the shock of his unwelcome attraction to her, the barely quelled rage of both combined.

He dragged his gaze over to meet hers, and the flash of her blue eyes twisted into him.

His words were low and tight. "You've been

making ties and cards instead of concentrating on schoolwork?"

She furrowed her brow. "Mr. Foley, Livie's out of school for the summer."

Mortified by not realizing that, he found a million other reasons to still be put out with the nanny.

"And what did you expect to accomplish by bringing her?"

She smiled oh-so innocuously. "Aside from the fact that you have a new tie, she wanted to wish you a Happy Father's Day. In person. Coming here was a gift to her, too."

Was this woman brazen enough to be pointing out his shortcomings to his face?

No one had dared before—not until *after* they were out of his employment.

Before he could erupt, she added, "We got a late start on driving, mostly because when I called your number, an assistant answered and said you wouldn't be home until after seven."

"Then you'd best get back to Austin, since it's a long ride."

She crossed her arms over her chest, and her agenda hit him square in the middle of the forehead.

"You set this up so I'd feel compelled to have you both overnight," he said. "Is that it?"

"I didn't think it'd be such an imposition. She's your daughter, not a nuisance."

He shook his head, ready to terminate her employment. But…

Dammit all, he didn't have time to go through another nanny search. He'd felt terrible enough after his daughter lost yet another caretaker. Besides, switching nannies so often did nothing for her structure, and Livie seemed to really be getting on well with this one.

But in the back of his thoughts, he

wondered if there was another reason he was hesitating to let Melanie Grandy go….

Hell no.

Not even remotely.

Still, as much as he didn't want to admit it, the nanny was right. It was the eve of Father's Day, and what kind of dad would he be to turn out his daughter?

Holding up a finger, he said, "One night, and I'm only agreeing to it because I don't want you driving Livie home in the dark all that way."

"Fair enough."

Maybe he should add more for good measure. "I'm extremely busy, and I don't want either of you underfoot."

Hollow, he thought. It all sounded as hollow as he felt.

"I understand," she said, her smile strained.

Then she turned around to retrieve two suitcases—one scuffed, one pristine.

Melanie Grandy's and Livie's baggage, he thought. But he wasn't about to let it become his own.

After entering, the nanny set the suitcases by the circular staircase, then immediately went to Livie. He took up the luggage, intending to get it out of the way and into the upstairs guest rooms, where he wouldn't have to look at it. His own bedroom was on the ground floor, so it would keep him removed, just the way he wanted it.

Yet, when he came back downstairs to hear his daughter and her nanny laughing about something or another on TV, he found himself walking toward them.

But then he changed direction, moving toward the sanctuary of his study.

But he could still hear them.

And weirdly enough, he kind of liked the sound.

Chapter Five

That night, Melanie couldn't sleep. Not with Zane Foley in the same townhouse.

She lay in the guest bedroom with the sheets tangled around her legs, trying to find a position that worked.

But she was restless, unable to stop thinking about him. And when she paired the stimulation of just being in the same pheromonal range as Zane Foley with the fact that she hadn't been intimate with a man for a long time, this resulted in one wide-awake woman.

For a while, she'd dated a Vegas bartender who nursed ambitions to open his own place, and the relationship had gotten serious enough, so that she'd developed what she'd believed could become serious feelings—at least until he dumped her. Otherwise, over the years, she spent her emotions wisely, knowing that sex didn't feel right unless there were fireworks during kisses, and dreams of being with that man for the rest of her life.

But thoughts of intimacy with a certain nearby boss weren't the only thing keeping her eyes wide-open tonight: it was also hard to wait until morning, when Father's Day would really arrive.

Boy, she hated having to plot and scheme like this, but she'd seen Zane Foley's eyes go gentle when Livie had given him that tie, and it had justified the chance Melanie had taken of losing her job altogether. However, if there'd been any sign of his closing himself entirely to Livie, Melanie would've cut the plan short and taken the little girl back home.

Yet, that hadn't been the case.

It was clear that Zane Foley loved his daughter and he didn't know how to show it. But Melanie wasn't so simple as to think that the situation could be changed in the course of one holiday, because Danielle's death had left too many scars.

As the grandfather clock downstairs struck twelve, Melanie sat up in bed. No use trying to sleep at all. Her mind and emotions were all over the place.

Maybe she could dig through his cupboard to see if he had any soothing tea?

Yeah. Right. Like he'd have tea. Yet, maybe

he'd have some milk. Soothing, good old milk worked every time.

Melanie crawled out of her guest bed, then adjusted her above-the-knee, rose-sprigged linen nightgown and headed for the door.

The clock stopped chiming as she crept down the hall past Livie's room, where Melanie peeked in to find the girl sprawled over the mattress, all relaxed knees and elbows.

Sleeping like a rock, as always, Melanie thought.

Warmth lodging in her upper chest, she shut the door and continued on her way. Down the circular stairs, quietly, slowly. Toward the kitchen.

But before she got there, she heard something in the living room. A wall blocked her view, but that didn't stop her from wondering if it was Zane.

Her heart butted against her chest.

Was he up, too?

She peered around the wall, but she must've already made some noise, because she saw him under the light of a dim Tiffany lamp, shoving some object into a small chest, his shoulders hunched.

Heart in her throat, she pulled back around the corner. Maybe she should go back to her bedroom and leave him alone.

Yet that was the last thing she really wanted—her body was very clear about that, too, as it began a sultry melt—hot, liquid, weak.

"Livie?" she heard him ask gruffly from the other room.

Shoot! No escaping now.

"No." Melanie realized she was wearing a nightgown. Conservative by most standards, but…a nightgown. Her breasts pressed against the linen, her nipples hardening at the sound of his voice alone.

But she couldn't hide here like a kid playing games.

Exhaling, she pulled her gown away from her chest, hoping that would do as she walked around the corner.

"It's me," she said. "I was going to the kitchen for something to drink, and I…"

He was staring at her, and it ratcheted her pulse up to high speed, enough so that she could feel the tiny, propulsive rhythm of it in her neck veins.

Just the two of us, she thought—*after midnight.*

While she'd been behind the wall, he'd clearly placed the wooden chest on a shelf to the side of his massive TV, but her mind wasn't so much on that, or even what might be inside of it.

One hundred percent of her was concentrated on *him.*

As he put his hands on his hips, making the muscles in his arms that much more obvious, making him seem like that noble, Western everyman, she corrected herself.

She was paying one hundred and ten percent attention to him now.

Those shoulders under his T-shirt, she thought. *And that broad chest...*

She bet that he had corrugated abs under his shirt, and she could just about feel them under her fingertips right now—ridges, muscle, flesh.

Hot and smooth...

"Sorry I bothered you," he said in a low voice that shook her, even over the quiet hum of everything else.

"No bother." What to say now? *Hi, yes, I'm sporting a nightgown, but you must admit it's prettier than that business suit you saw me wearing at our interviews.*

"You want me to…?" He motioned toward the kitchen, as if asking if he should fetch her something to drink.

My, how polite they suddenly were with each other.

"No, no, I've got it." She started to leave, thinking she would skip the beverage and just scram.

"Wait."

It was as if he had a pull on her, and she didn't go anywhere.

"Yes?" she said.

During his pause, she looked at him again, to find him running a slow gaze over her. When he saw that she noticed, he crossed his arms over his chest.

She was tingling all over. How could just a look do that?

"About earlier tonight…" he said, business as usual.

Great—did they have to talk about this now? "If you're going to fire me, could you do it tomorrow? I'd like to at least say goodbye to Livie—"

"I'm not going to fire you."

She stared at him as he leveled a firm gaze at her.

"Not yet, anyway," he added.

This man. Dear God, she couldn't make heads or tails of him. Was he angry because she'd brought Livie here, or not? After all, he'd retreated to his study right after they'd settled in; then they'd gone to bed after saying good-night. No more mention of anything. But she figured she would have to pay the piper when the timing was more convenient for him—like in the morning.

Yet, now she couldn't predict him at all.

He was as mysterious as whatever he'd put back in that chest by the TV.

"Then I'm glad you're not going to kick me out of the job," she said, gathering her guts, standing up for herself *and* for Livie. "I think I'm good for your daughter."

"I see that. She looks…happy." The corners of his mouth seemed to rise for a fleeting moment, then stopped as if his mouth was so unused to the expression that it rejected any change.

"She's happi*er*," Melanie said.

She waited for him to react, but he only got that shadowed look in his eyes again, the one she'd seen so many times during her interviews.

What could she do to get rid of it?

"You know what she'd really like?" Melanie asked.

"What?" The shadows were still there.

"If you'd do something with her tomorrow.

Even just lunch. Or, if you could spare any more time, she talks about trying some horseback riding. Maybe that'd be an activity you'd both like."

As if he'd been waiting for something to reject, he said, "Livie's grandma died from a riding accident. I'd prefer we didn't go that route."

Talk about stepping on a mine in a field full of them. "I'm sorry. I didn't know."

She hadn't come across any family history articles that went so deep beyond rumor and innuendo, and that family feud with the McCords.

"I try to keep most things private, if I can manage," he said. "Even from the press."

She thought of Danielle but didn't say anything. She didn't have to, when it looked as if those shadows were about to wrap around him and drag him into the walls.

"Instead of riding," she said, "how about an hour in the neighborhood park with us? I saw one about a block away."

He hesitated, and Melanie stabilized herself.

For Livie.

"She's missed you," she added. "This would mean the world to her."

When he glanced at that chest on the shelf, the tightening of his jaw made her think he was going to refuse the invitation. But then he started to walk away from the object, toward that hallway, as if leaving whatever was in the chest behind.

Or at least putting distance between him and it.

"One o'clock," he said as he continued toward the hallway, but she wasn't even sure she'd heard him right. "I have to go into Dallas before that, but I'll work the rest of the day from here."

"Did you say—?"

He paused, staring at the ground. "One o'clock."

Melanie could've shot through the roof. "Perfect. I'll pack a lunch, so don't worry about eating."

"You'll find the cupboards pretty empty around here," he said, meandering away again, barely looking at her. "Maybe I should leave money, if you don't mind stopping at the market."

"I don't mind. I don't mind at all."

She was smiling to beat the band, and he lifted his head, his gaze coming to rest on her mouth.

Then his eyes met hers again, thrashing her with a slam of that awareness she'd been trying so hard to dodge.

But dodge she did, nodding at him and then leaving before he could, walking past the kitchen and back to her bedroom, where she intended to shut the door nice and tight behind her until tomorrow.

He'd meant to get to the park for their Father's Day date.

He really had.

But Zane had found some accounting errors while reviewing a monthly report he was catching up on, and by the time he'd finished smoothing out the near damage, he'd looked at his watch to see that it was past three o'clock.

Three o'damned clock.

How had that happened?

He wanted to blame anyone but himself: why hadn't Melanie Grandy called him when he hadn't shown up at the park?

Yet, he figured the nanny had probably given up on him and hadn't bothered to even pick up the phone, because he had only confirmed that he was the worst dad in existence.

As his hand fell to his side, he wondered how Livie had taken his absence, but the answer wasn't hard to come by. She'd had plenty of practice at dealing with disappointment in him before, and he imagined that her opinion hadn't changed today.

And there it was—the exact reason he'd excused himself from bringing her up in the first place.

He called Monty to pick him up. When Monty arrived he didn't make any comments. Then again, unlike Melanie Grandy, the driver knew it wasn't his place to do so.

No, his employee only handed him a box after Zane had settled in the town car's backseat.

"What's this?" he asked Monty.

The driver pulled the vehicle away from the

valet station in the office building's parking structure. "Ms. Grandy sent it for you. She said she figured you might need it."

Steam fogged over him, an equal mix of disliking the position the nanny had put him in and...

God. He remembered last night, when she'd been standing there in her nightie. Even though the sleepwear had been modest, it had shown more leg than he'd ever seen of her.

Long, lean leg. And he'd wanted to go to Melanie Grandy, bend down to curl his fingers around her ankle, then start from there on up, skimming over her toned calf, the soft, damp back of her knee, higher....

But he'd barred himself from doing any of it, mostly because of what he'd stowed in the chest just before he'd heard her moving around while going to the kitchen.

Danielle's ashes in an urn.

He supposed that the approaching anniversary of his first wife's suicide had urged him to take out her remains. But then again, he often contemplated her—the memories of what he could've done. The penance for not being able to stop her…

In any case, he'd been in a brooding mood, and the nanny had broken it open for a short time before he'd told himself to get out of the room, to resist a situation he just couldn't handle.

Now he looked at the box she had sent for him to open, and like that chest, he wished he could just keep it closed.

But since he had a feeling about what was inside, he took off the lid.

The R2-D2 tie.

He tossed the box lid to the seat. *Damn that woman.* She'd probably found it where he'd placed it on the kitchen counter last night.

Legs or not, she was making his life hell.

Zane caught Monty's gaze in the rearview mirror just before the driver looked away.

The rest of the ride was like a session in a torture chamber, with the world's most invisible, cutting, self-inflicted weapons. Zane went back and forth between cursing himself for blowing it with Livie today and thinking that he should just send her back home, until Monty pulled up to his townhouse, with its luxurious, sleek façade that didn't offer even a hint of the darkness inside.

They would be waiting in there for him: Livie, with those eyes that slayed Zane every time he saw them. And Melanie Grandy— who had quite a way of killing him softly, too.

Dammit.

He took off his Armani tie and put on the R2-D2 one, feeling like an ass, but not just because he was wearing a cartoon character on his chest.

Then Zane got out of the car, held up a hand to thank Monty and watched his driver pull away in a stream of red taillights.

He ran a hand through his hair, took a deep breath and entered his home, thinking that he'd never been so cautious about coming into his own doggone place before the nanny had arrived.

Standing in the foyer, he set down his briefcase, listening for any signs of life. No TV. No clanging around in the kitchen.

He went back outside to check the stand-alone garage, to see if Melanie's designated Tall Oaks Volvo was still there where he'd parked it for her, last night before retiring.

Present and accounted for.

When he wandered back inside, ready to capitulate and call her cell phone, he heard something floating down from the stairway.

Laughter.

The roof terrace, he thought, his veins going taut as he took in the sound. It rang through him, and for a forbidden moment, he allowed it to settle.

What would it be like to have a house that sounded like this all the time?

Then reality returned. He had to go up to the roof, and the minute they saw him the laughter would stop.

Okay, you're a man, he told himself. *Face the consequences.*

He straightened the R2-D2 tie and climbed the stairs, following the laughter—actually drawn to it, as he'd been last night, when it had filled this house.

When it had even filled something else that he wasn't sure he could define.

Arriving at the roof, he found them sitting in lounge chairs that faced the Dallas skyline. The river sparkled in the late afternoon sunshine.

They'd turned on the small rock waterfall near the hot tub, and the splash of it mingled with Melanie's voice as she told Livie some story about a time she'd gone waterskiing.

"I never drank so much water as I did that day on the lake," she said at the end of her tale. "I had a stomachache for hours afterward."

Livie was giggling and sipping from a straw in a glass that looked to be full of milk. Her gaze was fixed on her nanny, as if she were the most incredible thing to drop from the sky since stardust.

As Zane watched them, *his* stomach ached with something sharp and empty stabbing it.

When was the last time Livie had looked at him that way?

Last night, he thought. And he hadn't returned the affection.

Worst father ever, he thought again, taking no pride in this accomplishment.

He felt like such a nothing, all he wanted to do was change the perception—even if it were just for the final hours of Father's Day.

He cleared his throat and both females looked back, Livie watching him, her gaze wounded.

And Melanie?

She was watching him, too, but she looked about ready to throttle him. Yet, how could he be offended when she was angry for the sake of his daughter?

"I apologize," he said, "for missing our date. I lost track of time."

The excuse didn't hold any water at all. In fact, with the way the nanny was visually shooting bullets at him, his words seemed punctured.

He continued. "Livie, I know how much you wanted me there."

Her gaze had come to rest on his tie. That darn R2-D2-riddled tie.

And lo and behold, she smiled. An injured smile, to be sure, but at least he'd done something right today.

Thanks to Melanie, he reluctantly admitted to himself.

The nanny saw the tie, too, but that didn't change her expression. "We understand. Work's important."

Yes, it is, he wanted to say, but he didn't. It didn't seem so true right now.

They were both still sitting in their lounge chairs, their bodies slanted toward the skyline, as if they knew better than to commit to turning all the way toward him.

"We had fun, Daddy," Livie said. "Ms. Grandy made peanut butter and jelly starfish sandwiches. And we shared oranges with Sheree and Tammy."

Zane almost flinched. Even after what he'd done, his daughter was still talking to him as if he hadn't screwed up?

"Sheree and Tammy are neighbor girls," the nanny said, grinning at Livie. "Their mom told me that they're six and seven years old, almost twins with Livie."

"And they have American Girl dolls, too!" his daughter added.

They laughed again, and Zane wished he could join in.

But he could—couldn't he?

Even though he wondered, he knew that he would have to make it up to Livie somehow, because having her go back to Austin just after he'd pulled the rug out from under her was unthinkable.

Distance was fine, he told himself. It was subtle. But this afternoon he'd done something cruel—and he even wondered if he'd done it subconsciously, because he knew that going to the park would lead to daytrips and that would lead to week-long trips, and…

He stopped himself, vowing to give them a great night instead. Afterward, they could all go back to where they belonged, feeling the better for it.

"We're going to do something else right now," he said. "So why don't you get yourselves up so we can go?"

Now Livie swung her legs to the side of her chair, and Zane smiled.

"Where're we going, Daddy?"

"To a place that'll make you real happy. Trust me on that."

As his daughter clapped her hands, he couldn't help but notice that Melanie wasn't applauding at all.

Melanie had always told herself that she couldn't be bought off, but as she stood in front of the mirror of the personal shopper's boutique in Westenra's, a high-class department store in the swanky Garden Faire Mall, she wasn't so sure.

"Gorgeous," said the sales associate as she adjusted the skirt of the sea-blue cocktail dress that Melanie was trying on. "It compliments your eyes, hair and skin tone. You look like a movie star!"

In back of Melanie, Livie glanced up from her picture book from where she was sitting on the leather sofa. Zane had already bought her a bunch of stuff at a bookstore.

"Oh, Ms. Grandy," Livie said. "You're bea-u-ti-ful."

Melanie smiled at her while avoiding looking at Zane, who was sitting right next to his daughter.

"We'll take this last dress, too," he said.

Ecstatic at the commission she'd rung up, the personal shopper scooped up the six other outfits her client had tried on and flitted off, leaving Melanie alone in the mirror.

She tried not to give in to the lure of all this, but at the sight of herself she went a little dreamy. She looked like she'd found a glass slipper, but like Cinderella at the stroke of midnight, she knew this was only transient.

Still…

Zane Foley seemed to catch her doubt. "That dress is all yours, if you want, just like the other outfits you've tried on."

Yes, she wanted. And…*darn him, he knew*. She could tell from the contented way he was sitting there, taking it all in, as if this made up for his ditching Livie this afternoon.

Melanie ran her hand over the silk of the dress's haltered neckline. It wasn't that she didn't believe he'd lost track of time at the office. Oh, yes, she *truly* had faith in that. And that was the problem.

He would always lose track at the expense of Livie unless something was done about it.

Turning around, she faced him, and once again she was thrown off by his mere presence. The dark hair that seemed slightly ruffled from a long day. The hazel eyes that were even now stroking over her and making her get butterflies in her tummy.

And the R2-D2 tie.

He was still wearing it, and she couldn't help but appreciate that, even if she'd pushed it on him.

"Mr. Foley, I don't think—"

"Stop with the polite refusals," he said. "As Livie's nanny, you need to look the part."

"You already told me that."

She shot him a glance that said the rest: *and this has no connection to how you win over people? With how you buy Livie all those dolls instead of showing up to be with her every once in a while?*

She couldn't say it out loud. Not with Livie here, even if the child had gone back to reading her books.

"Besides," Melanie continued, "I'm guessing that Livie and I probably won't be attending many cocktail parties together."

He leaned forward, and as those butterflies painted the lining of her belly with flutters, she almost touched her stomach, calming them.

Chasing them away.

"Okay, maybe I'm aiming for more than appearances," he said quietly.

He left it at that.

But what did he mean? Was he using these dresses as a means to thank her for what she'd done for Father's Day?

She searched his gaze for more of a hint,

and when she didn't find any, she looked further for a shade of dishonesty.

None of that either, but she had to turn back to the mirror, because he made her feel like a hypocrite.

Talk about dishonesty.

She ran a hand down the dress. Classy—so unlike the former showgirl or lower-class daughter whose family skimmed the poverty line.

But even in this dress, the old days still seemed to cling to Melanie, refusing to let go, no matter how hard she was trying.

The secret of her past levered down on her as, in the mirror, she saw Zane Foley come to a stand. He whispered something to Livie, and the girl sprang to her feet, clutching her books.

"We'll be back soon," he said as he began walking away with his daughter.

Melanie gave him a quizzical look in the mirror.

He smiled, and it ripped through her, upending every cell in its wake.

"We're headed for the pièce de résistance," he said, glancing down at Livie, who gazed back at him adoringly. "There's a massive Toys 'R' Us store that rivals the one in Times Square, and I thought Livie might have some fun there."

"But…" Melanie began.

By now, his daughter was tugging him away, and he actually seemed amused by that.

"Don't worry," he said. "You'll be busy here."

As Livie pulled him out of the boutique, the personal shopper returned, seeming so chipper that it almost scared Melanie.

"Are you ready?" the woman asked.

Melanie wasn't sure if she liked this or not. "For what?"

The other woman laughed, almost sounding like one of those twittering birds who'd created Cinderella's dress in the Disney movie.

"You've got a makeover waiting for you, ma'am."

Melanie's pulse leaped before she tamed it.

A…makeover?

She glanced in the mirror again, and instead of seeing the present, she thought back to a girl who used to wear drab dresses, the young woman who'd worked hard to get where she was today.

A makeover.

How could she refuse?

Chapter Six

When Melanie called Zane's cell to tell him that her makeover appointment was done, he made sure Monty had all the toys Livie had purchased in hand.

Then, since Livie begged to go with Monty to the parked car where she could begin to tear into her new toys, Zane let her escape the tedium of the department store and headed there alone so he could settle the bill while their packages were carried to the valet station.

Hopefully, he thought after rapidly taking care of money matters and boarding the Up escalator, *this shopping trip and makeover would improve Melanie's mood.* If so, he would look forward to getting back to the townhouse with a more chipper nanny, then prepare to say goodbye to her and his daughter in the morning.

A niggle got to him, but he didn't pay any mind to it.

Yup, they'd be gone tomorrow, and life would go back to normal.

He came to the personal shopper's boutique, where Melanie had evidently gone to put on one of her new outfits with the sales associate's encouragement. When he got there, a few women were in front of the mirror, flittering about and doing what women often did over new clothes.

Zane had just opened his mouth to ask if his

employee was set to leave when the women parted to reveal the nanny in the midst of them.

The words lodged in his chest, then began pumping like a conflicting heartbeat.

Melanie?

Her blond hair was swept back into a graceful chignon, which complemented the slim lines of a short jacket and long cigarette skirt worthy of Jackie O. Her makeup was elegant, bringing out the breathtaking blue of her eyes and the lovely heart shape of her face.

She fit the role of a princess, not a nanny, and for a taboo instant, he envisioned her on his arm at a charity event, shining like the brightest of stars.

Seconds must've passed. Maybe even minutes. And during each escalating heart-beat, he kept himself from saying something he would regret to this new woman, even if, under the makeup and clothing, she was still the same lady who'd hooked his attention that first day.

She just had an extra sparkle in her eyes, and that was what took his breath away.

She was staring right back at him with something that resembled hope as she folded her hands in front of her—a nervous gesture he was just starting to recognize.

Melanie, he thought. Not "the nanny."

Not now.

"You…" He trailed off.

Surely he could find a comment somewhere in his brain. Any comment. Zane Foley was the last man on earth who should've been searching for words.

A couple of the sales associates laughed softly, and heat crept up Zane's neck.

He pushed his hands into his suit pockets as

he addressed his employee. "Looks as if you're ready."

His back-to-business tone seemed to bring Melanie—no, it *had* to remain "the nanny"—back to reality, too. But as she nodded at him, then thanked the women around her, he could tell that she'd lost the glimmer that had made her more beautiful than ever, and he hated that he'd done this to her.

But what was new?

He turned to leave, getting the hell out of there, and she caught up just as they were crossing the marble floors and coming to the baby grand piano near the escalators. The musician was playing that song from *Casablanca.*

He hoped she didn't notice.

"But," she said, "I didn't tip them yet."

"It's taken care of."

Without looking at her, he motioned for

her to climb aboard the Down escalator before him.

Cold, he thought. Didn't he have it within himself to be more than that?

She got on the conveyance, turning around to face him while holding the moving handrail. "But shouldn't I—?"

"It was my treat. Besides, I know the owners and my credit's good with them."

"Oh." She patted the side of her hairdo, as if not knowing what else to do. "Of course you know them. You probably know every top tax-bracket entrepreneur in the country."

"I know them because I helped develop this center, among others that Westenra's also uses."

At the news, she went silent, as if he'd intentionally reminded her of his station in life and hers—and the chasm between them.

But he hadn't meant to.

Even so, the sudden space between them bothered Zane. God knew why, because it wasn't as if they would ever be close.

They got off the escalator and moved through the men's shoe department toward the exit where Monty would be waiting. Zane couldn't help noticing that the suit-and-tie salesmen were watching Melanie Grandy, and he wanted to take her arm and link it through his in a show of…

He stopped himself before he used the word *"possession."*

Not him. Not for her.

Nevertheless, he didn't appreciate the staring, so he shot the men subtle *back-off* looks, while approaching the doors to the valet and pickup area.

When they got out there, Monty hadn't yet arrived, and Zane guessed it was because Livie was probably going through her new purchases and making it nearly impossible for the softhearted driver to get the packages in the trunk.

He would give them three more minutes before calling.

As they waited, a couple of valets were giving Melanie the eye, just as the guys inside had been doing. With one extra long look at them, Zane persuaded the boys to go back to being valets instead of slobbering dogs.

Melanie didn't seem to notice any of it. She stood there, face forward, the silence deafening.

Luckily, she broke it.

"And how did Toys 'R' Us go with Livie?" she asked.

In spite of himself, a smile captured his mouth, and when it stayed, it surprised him a little. "She was really excited. They had a Ferris wheel in the middle of the store. We went on that thing three times."

"Good." A smile broke out over her face, too.

My, wasn't she content about her schemes to get father and daughter together?

Her happiness would end soon enough when she realized that tonight wasn't going anywhere beyond this.

He shifted under the weight of the thought—and under the heft of the tension that remained between them.

But she still seemed to be in a positive mood. She even laughed a bit, yet it sounded more self-aware than anything.

"What is it?" he asked.

She gestured to her dress, her face and hair. "This whole night. Me getting made over at your pleasure."

He almost coughed.

She caught herself. "That's not exactly what I meant." Sighing, she shook her head. "I don't know. Maybe it has something to do with… Well, I heard that you make sure all the Foley nannies have looked good to one extent or another."

What was this about? "Meaning…?" he asked.

"Rumor has it that in the past most nannies were easy on the eye."

That heat began its slow crawl up his skin again, from his neck to his face. "And who told you this?"

"You're not confirming or denying my comment."

He knew she wouldn't give up her source, and even though that got to him, he also had to respect her loyalty. It was a decent quality for anyone to have. Besides, if he really cared about the mild gossip that much, he could narrow it down to one of a few other employees with whom she had regular contact.

"Pretty has nothing to do with it," he muttered. "It's never been a job requirement."

And that was the truth. Even now, he couldn't say if the other nannies had been good looking or not. All he knew was that Melanie Grandy affected him like none of the others had, and it didn't sit well.

"If appearances don't matter," she said, "then why give me a makeover, even as a thank you?"

She'd turned to him in her direct manner. He faced her, too, and out of habit, he actually thought he might be able to make her look away if he stayed quiet long enough.

Yet she stood her ground, and he was the one at the disadvantage, overtaken by the depth and color of her eyes. There was a vivid strength in her gaze, like the undertow of the sea, and he'd noticed it even prior to the makeup bringing it out.

Before he knew what he was doing, he raised his hand and rested it on her cheek, where there had always been a natural blush, even without the aid of all these cosmetics.

Then, realizing what had just happened, he rubbed his thumb over the makeup as if to take some of it off.

"You don't need all this," he said.

And it was true. Achingly true.

Her eyes had gone wide. He'd shocked her, he knew, and he wondered if it was because of his brash move or because she could feel the same current that sizzled when his skin met hers.

He could see her throat working as she swallowed, and his breathing picked up.

What if he moved his fingertips down over her jaw, to her neck, where he could brush over the delicate, smooth lines? What would she do then?

What would *he* do after that?

Nothing around them stirred, the air seeming to hover in place, locking everything in to this one moment, this one touch. Locking them into each other's gazes, where he could see a different world, a livelier one, hued with the laughter he'd heard on the roof of his townhouse a few hours ago.

But then he remembered how he'd put an end to the gaiety, just because he was Zane Foley—bad husband, bad father.

He'd promised he wouldn't add any more "bad"s to his list.

Slowly, he removed his hand from her face and turned away, going for his cell phone to see where in tarnation Monty was.

As he accessed speed dial, he could feel Melanie beside him, awkward in the aftermath. And he hated himself for doing that to her— putting this otherwise self-assured woman in a place where she had no firm footing.

That's right, he thought, *once again Zane Foley's made a mess of things.*

But he was going to make sure it didn't happen again.

Ever.

Melanie arose early the next morning, getting out of bed at the crack of dawn.

Since sleep hadn't come easy—*once again*—she thought she might as well make the most of her last morning here. So she showered and threw on a sundress before going down to the kitchen, where she'd stored all the food she'd purchased from the market yesterday, including the makings of a meal that had been a hit with kids in the past— fluffy biscuit sandwiches teeming with egg, bacon and cheese. Hearty and filling.

As the biscuits baked in the oven, she began whisking the eggs, milk, garlic salt and pepper together, but all the while she kept looking toward the hallway that led to Zane's study and bedroom.

Couldn't she stop thinking of how he'd touched her last night? How her heart had nearly exploded at the feel of his hand on her cheek?

She stopped taking her frustration out on the eggs and fanned a hand in front of her face. *Whoo.* Maybe it was the heat of the oven, combined with the vulnerability of her skin after last night's makeover facial.

Or maybe it was because Zane Foley had a power over her that no man had ever come close to.

Either way, he'd pulled away from her in the end, sending her belly sinking. Because… seriously?

She and Zane Foley—the *billionaire?*

Chuffing, she told herself that he'd just been

wiping makeup off her face, and that was that. He was a control freak, and that obviously extended to making sure his nannies were just the way he wanted to see them, if anyone should ever get a gander.

But…

She closed her eyes. How about the desire she'd seen in his gaze? At least, that's what she thought it'd been when it'd just about buckled her knees.

She opened her eyes again, wishing she could figure him all the way out.

Her gaze wandered to the living room, where he'd been looking at something in that chest the other night.

What if she took a peek, just in case it offered an answer?

Any answer.

Glancing around at the still house, with its blur of stained glass muting the morning, she put down the egg bowl before second guessing herself, then went to the living room, heading straight for the TV and the chest sitting on the shelves right beside it.

All while, she chided herself. *Mel, think about what you're doing.*

But if this helped her to understand him, it couldn't hurt, right?

She unlatched the chest—there was no lock, thank goodness—then eased it open to get a glimpse.

What she found made her close it and put it back the way she'd found it, her heartbeat strangled.

An urn.

Danielle's ashes?

Feeling as if she'd intruded into someone's most private secrets, Melanie retreated back to the kitchen to finish making breakfast.

She should've known that was what Zane

had been hunched over the other night. If they *were* Danielle's ashes—and Melanie would bet on the truth of that—he kept his deceased wife close. Physically close, not just mentally or emotionally. Six years, and he hadn't let her go for even a few yards.

No wonder he had that darkness in his eyes: because the shadow still resided in his house.

She stared at the mess on the counter, the bowls and ingredients fuzzing before her. If she'd entertained any thoughts of Zane's interest in her before, they were beaten down now. After all, how could she compete with a woman who would always be here?

And just who had this woman been, to have such a hold on him?

She heard a door opening upstairs, then footsteps treading down the steps. When Livie came around the corner, her hair tousled from sleep, Melanie motioned her over for a good-morning hug.

No one should have to compete with a ghost, Melanie thought as the little girl smiled and rubbed her eyes, coming to her nanny. Not Livie and not...

Well, not anyone else.

She heard another person enter the kitchen from the opposite direction, and her pulse kicked.

Then his voice.

"I thought I smelled something good," he said as Melanie and Livie parted.

His daughter got that shy grin on her face, as if she were wondering whether or not to go to her daddy. But out of the corner of Melanie's eye, she saw him bend down—an invitation for the child to come on over.

It was an improvement, she thought, taking the biscuits out of the oven.

The embrace between father and daughter was tentative, but it was a start. And as he finished hugging her, keeping a light hold on her pajamas as she drew away, Melanie became acutely aware that he was in a pair of sweats and a T-shirt, just like the other night.

All that was missing was her nightgown and the tick of a clock while they looked at each other from across the living room.

"Morning," he said.

"Morning." She sent a quick glance of acknowledgement over her shoulder, intending to get right to work again.

But when Livie came back over to Melanie and leaned her sleepy head against her leg, Nanny Workhorse lost direction.

And it only got worse when Zane's gaze fell on her and Livie, a look of such longing about him that, for a brief moment, it made her want to cry.

Such a strong, solid man, she thought, and to see a crack in his defenses made her want to reach out.

Made her want to make him happy.

"Hey, Livie," she said, resting a hand on the child's head. "Breakfast is coming right up. Maybe you and Daddy can sit at the table and start drinking your orange juice together. He'll have to get to work soon."

Zane's eyes met hers, and along with the zing of electricity that always came with it, she also noticed a bared gratefulness.

She grinned and nodded toward a cabinet that she knew contained the glasses. He understood, going to it, getting three out.

Three, not just two.

But the plan was to get *them* together, and the last thing Melanie wanted to do was act as the go-between she'd been for the last couple of days. They should relate to each other without her around, just as they had at the toy store last night.

"Mr. Foley," she said, "I need to eat on the fly while I pack up for Livie and myself."

She could feel Livie grip her leg, but Melanie stroked the girl's hair, soothing her. They would have to leave sooner or later.

"I see," he said. Then he set the glasses on the counter.

Livie spoke up. "We can't stay another day? Not even so we can listen to the band in the park tonight in the hot tub?"

Livie and Melanie had found fliers advertising a family group playing in the nearby park that night during a farmer's market. And since Zane's townhouse was so close, they would probably be able to hear its amplified sound from his roof, where the little girl had been begging Melanie to try the spa.

He'd braced his hands on the counter, and

Melanie could tell he was fighting with himself.

Help him, she thought.

"We don't have any pressing engagements in Austin," she said, giving him an opening. "And the maintenance crew can do work inside the house while we're not around."

Finally, he slid her one of those looks— pulled apart by two different, warring sides.

The dad versus the haunted man.

Melanie silently tried to lend him encouragement. *Please,* she thought. *Do it for Livie.*

He opened the fridge, took out the juice, then began to pour. "All right. You can stay another night then. But I've got work."

Success!

"Yes, you do," Melanie said as Livie hugged her nanny's leg.

Melanie squeezed the little girl's shoulder, smiling down at her. Because after tonight, when they went back to Austin, smiles would probably come few and far between.

Melanie had spent the day seeing that Livie kept to her schedule while her dad was at the office.

After a morning full of dance and drawing, they'd picnicked in the park again, watching tonight's event being set up. Then they'd gone to a nearby café, where Livie had enjoyed the "adult experience" of drinking tea, then climbing on one of the rented computers to play some phonics games that Melanie had read about in a child-care magazine.

As her charge was doing her thing, Melanie went on her own computer, making sure Livie didn't see the subject of her Internet search.

Danielle Foley.

However, about an hour later, Melanie didn't know a whole lot more than she'd started with. It seemed that Danielle had shunned the press, just as her husband did. But Melanie *had* been able to uncover a few links to high school reunion sites, and there she'd been able to get a few more tidbits about the woman who still seemed to be such a presence in the Foley lives.

Although any hints about Danielle's death had been vague, Melanie had seen a few pictures of someone who resembled Livie so much that it was eerie: the same dark eyes and hair, the same gentle expressions of disappointment floating over every feature.

Melanie had also pulled up some articles about bipolar disorder, and by the time she was done, Livie was ready to go.

Doing her best to act as if the research hadn't bothered her, Melanie asked Livie to help her put together a dinner of beef tostadas and fruit salad.

But it was hard to keep her mind off Danielle, especially with Livie—her miniature double—right here. Melanie could see how the resemblance to her mom might affect Zane, could see that he must've been crushed by Danielle's passing to still keep her so close.

Again, she thought that his grief must be so strong that he chose to avoid his daughter.

A dull throb beat through her chest, but she ignored it until Zane came home, joining them on the roof terrace while the band kicked into gear at the nearby park, lending the warm air graceful notes.

As the group played "Waltzing Matilda," Melanie laid out Zane's and Livie's meals, then started back to the kitchen to eat hers while the other two did more bonding. She would go up there again soon, so Zane could retreat to his study and she could supervise Livie in the hot tub.

"Hey," Zane said from his seat at the glass-topped table, as she made her way through the sliding doors. "Where're you going?"

She smiled. "You two enjoy the music. I've got things to—"

Now Livie turned her big eyes on her nanny.

Both of them were watching Melanie. They seemed so forlorn, even with their meals sitting there in front of them. Despite that food on the table, the scene somehow looked empty.

Zane stood, pulling out a chair. "We'd enjoy your company."

As he waited, she could see herself with them, a part of the family, and she only wished it could be real.

"Ms. Grandy?" Zane asked, his voice softly raking over her skin, destroying every "but" she could think of.

"All right," she said, grinning at Livie. "Just let me get my plate."

She left, catching father and daughter as they traded smiles.

Had they talked about how she had been missing during breakfast? *Nah,* she thought, gathering her stuff and climbing the stairs again. Although maybe their nanny was the only subject they had in common right now.

The very idea made her sad, so after she joined them, she made a real effort to introduce subjects that would help them to connect: Livie's uncles, her schoolwork, her favorite things about both Austin and Dallas.

Zane listened intently to all of it, even smiling sometimes at the cuteness that was Livie. And the little girl ate that right up.

By the end of the meal, Melanie thought it was time well spent—a great springboard for their relationship.

But then it happened.

"I love Mexican food," Livie said, nearing the last of her tostada. "You make it yummy, Ms. Grandy."

"Thank you."

She could feel Zane's gaze on her again, and goose bumps shivered over her. Actually, she'd felt his attention throughout dinner, but she couldn't stop from picturing how he'd probably once looked at Danielle, too, back when they had first fallen in love.

Yet Melanie kept telling herself that the way he felt about his wife was none of a nanny's business, even if she found herself wishing that it were.

Livie was still talking. "Cook says that Mommy liked this kind of food." She paused. "Didn't she, Daddy?"

It was as if a cold wind had come off the river and frozen Zane in his seat. After a second that lasted way too long, he wiped his mouth with his napkin. The gesture was controlled, so very careful.

Then he said, "Yes, she did, Livie."

But he changed the subject back to his daughter's schooling so quickly that Melanie almost got whiplash. Then, after finishing the rest of his food, he excused himself, heading for the sliding-glass door.

Just as Melanie was about to despair, he seemed to reconsider, coming over to touch Livie's shoulder, her cheek.

Then, averting his gaze, he left.

Melanie gauged Livie's reaction, but the child was quietly finishing her tostada without as much as a second glance to where her father had deserted her yet again.

Without thinking, Melanie wrapped an arm around her and kissed her forehead.

Livie just kept eating, not even acknowledging her nanny.

Yet Melanie still hugged the girl, unwilling to let go.

One step forward, two steps back, she thought.

And, at this moment, she couldn't imagine how it would ever be any different with Zane Foley.

Chapter Seven

The sunlight descended through the windows of Zane's study, casting stained-glass reflections as he sat in his desk chair.

He told himself to go back to the roof, to tell Livie not only that her mom had loved Mexican food, but that she had collected porcelain figurines that she'd talked about giving their daughter someday. He wanted to relate how her mother had also loved a nice, old-fashioned scary movie, like those you would've gone to at a drive-in. He wanted to let Livie know that, on some afternoons, Danielle had ridden her bike around the Dallas estate they used to live on before Zane had sold the place to move here, by himself.

And on the days that the sun would shine over the Texas landscape, as well as within Danielle, she'd driven that bike to a park—her favorite—where she would sit on a tiny bridge while a stream burbled just underneath her dangling feet.

But those had been on her good days.

Sometimes Zane couldn't separate the positive stories from the negative, because, looking back, it all seemed to fade together— good days into bad—like a blurred canvas of memory.

He leaned forward in his chair, digging his fingers through his hair. *Damn you, Danielle,* he thought. *Damn you for leaving her…me… alone to live this way.*

Glancing up, he saw the portrait of Livie.

His daughter was just upstairs, and so was Melanie—a woman whose smiles came so easily, without any threat of a cost to them later.

Or that's how it seemed, anyway.

So it was tempting, very damned tempting, to go back up there, because there were times when Melanie almost made him forget. Maybe not entirely, but she did cause him to think that he could learn to live beyond the past.

At least that much had been true for the last couple of days, when he'd caught himself thinking that there might be a little light ahead.

Yet, he also knew other things were ahead of him, too—namely the anniversary of Danielle's death.

Just over one week away.

The thought pinned him to his chair, and he didn't go back upstairs. Instead, he awakened his computer and sought work, a refuge.

His eternal saving grace.

Since Zane had retired to that study of his, Melanie didn't expect to see him for the rest of the night. So after dinner, she and Livie got into the bathing suits they'd purchased in a superstore during their market run yesterday, then eased into the hot tub.

As always, Livie seemed to leave her father behind and, bit by bit, get into the moment. Melanie made it easier for her by initiating a skirmish with bottled bubbles they'd also purchased, blowing the balls of soap at each other through the wands. It got Livie to giggling, until they both settled down to listen to the last of the music from the band in the park, the tunes floating away into the night.

Deciding they'd had enough for the time being, Melanie got Livvie out of the tub and ready for bed, tucking the girl in before reading her a story about The Three Little Pigs.

Halfway through, she heard Livie's breathing even out, and Melanie closed the book, glancing beside her to where the child lay, her eyes closed, her lashes long and angelic.

Dreamland, she thought, grateful that Livie's tendency to sleep deeply provided her a haven of sorts. The hot tub had probably even relaxed her further.

Melanie rested her hand on her charge's arm, closing her eyes, too, smiling. She was so lucky to be here.

Best job in the world.

She must've floated off, because after she opened her eyes, kissed Livie's cheek, shut off the light, then went to her own room,

Melanie's travel clock read about an hour later than when she'd put Livie to bed.

Still, it was pretty early yet, and she thought it might be nice to stay up, maybe watch some TV downstairs, then crawl into bed.

But was Zane in his study? Would she run into him down there?

Thinking of her boss brought the end of dinner rushing back. Livie had only asked a simple question about Danielle, and Zane had withdrawn into himself yet again. Although he'd made progress with his daughter recently, he'd sure hit a wall tonight. And when Melanie thought of how Livie had gotten quiet right after he left, frustration burned deep inside again.

This had to end, Melanie thought, and if there was a chance that she could get Zane Foley to come around even a little more before they left for Austin tomorrow, she should take it.

Dedicated to what she would do now instead of watching TV, she decided that she would make *sure* she ran into him downstairs.

She was wearing one of her modest nightgowns, but among the new outfits Zane had purchased for her she'd found a robe that she hadn't tried on at the department store. He must've requested one from the personal shopper on the sly. Melanie wondered if he'd done so because he took offense to her scampering around in her nightgown.

But she could've sworn that offense was not what she had seen on his face that night when he had lavished a hot, long look over her body, making her tremble.

She slipped into the white silk, tying the sash around her waist, pausing at the elegant feel of the material.

So tasteful, she thought. This wasn't the

type of robe girls like Melanie Grandy wore.
Sure, she'd fit well enough with those sequins
and feathers on that Vegas stage, but this was
the real thing, not an act.

Then it struck her that, by keeping her past
from everyone, her whole life was an act, and
she pulled the robe closer around her, heading
for her boss's study to complete her mission
as Livie's advocate.

She would talk to him and get out of his
hair. In and out.

When she saw that his light was on behind
the door, she ventured a knock.

After a moment, she heard him.

"Yes?"

"It's me. May I come in?"

A hesitation.

Heck, she could almost imagine him
cursing at having to deal with her, because he
had to know what this was about.

"Door's unlocked," he finally said.

Heart thudding—it always did that Pavlovian trick when she heard Zane Foley—she opened the door to find him facing toward her at his desk, his computer on, the screen tilted toward the doorway enough to show a picture of the Santa Magdalena Diamond. He kept his eyes on it.

What do you know, she thought, *he's working.*

She shut the door behind her and he looked up, sitting straight, his jaw tensing.

The nightgown, she thought. *The robe.*

She pulled the silk robe even tighter around her, but the whisper of it against her skin only made her realize that the hairs on her arms were standing at attention.

"I'm sorry for bothering you," she said, "but I thought we might have a word, since Livie's down for the count."

He tore his gaze away from her, and she actually reveled in the effort it seemed to take.

But she shouldn't be reveling with him.

"I can guess what this is about," he said, pressing a button on his keyboard, shutting down the machine.

"Then it's no surprise I'm here."

"Ms. Grandy," he said, finally glancing at her again, but this time he was all coolness. "I'm never surprised when you approach me on Livie's behalf. But you don't seem to remember something I told you during our second interview."

"I remember. You told me advice wasn't appreciated."

"So why do I have the feeling you're about to give me some anyway?"

She forgot about the robe and approached his desk. "Do you realize what it's like to sit by and watch her suffer? If I *didn't* say anything, I'd never forgive myself. I'm only too glad to overstep my bounds."

He rose from his chair, and she couldn't help but think of a pillar of fire. His eyes certainly had a flare to them.

She pressed on. "Is it *that* painful for you to give Livie even some indication of what her mother was like? She has no idea, and more than anything, she wants to know. A child needs a mom, whether or not she's actually there."

"That'll be enough."

"No, this isn't *nearly* enough." Her emotions were spilling out of her; she'd held on to them so tightly that she couldn't stop them now that she'd uncorked herself. "Livie's got a heart of gold, but she's buried it so deep that I wonder how long it'll be before she can't find it altogether. People have a tendency to shove their feelings away when they're rejected over and over again, and one day, you're going to find that's what happened to your daughter." She took a deep breath, exhaled. "If you're around to see it."

"I will be ar—" He cut himself off, and she wasn't sure if it was because he didn't deign to have this conversation or if he didn't know how to respond.

He hid whatever it was well, but then again, he always did.

She started to talk again, but he drilled her with a glare while beginning to come around the desk with such a deliberate pace that her adrenaline raced through her, prodding her to back away, to run.

But she stayed, even if she was getting pummeled by her heartbeat.

"I've seen how much you love Livie," she said, her voice sounding tangled. She tried to recover. "So I just can't understand why you constantly push her back. Why you push—"

Pressing her lips together, she saved herself just before she said "—*everyone back.*"

He'd rounded the desk by now, coming to stand only a foot away. Tall, overbearing.

She raised her face to meet his intense gaze, and anything else she might've added to her impassioned diatribe only disappeared, taken over by the brutal pounding of her blood in her veins.

"If you have more for me," he said, low and contained over a fierceness she knew he was keeping in check, "put it on the table."

She wanted to. Lord knows she did. But since this discussion had seemed to go beyond his daughter now, how could she keep lecturing him on shortcomings when she had so many herself?

He was so close that she could smell the soap on his skin—fresh and manly, like he'd lathered himself after a hard day of work. She could imagine him under the pelting force of a shower, his skin bare….

Her mind got fuzzy, her judgment was gone.

And when he leaned even nearer, daring her again to keep on talking, she reached for the desk, knowing it was the only thing that could hold her up.

Yet, like her, he seemed to have lost his train of thought.

He was so close she could feel his breath on her face.

So close that all she would have to do was—

It was as if something had pushed her forward, and she canted toward him, pressing her lips to his, knowing it was wrong but unable to stop herself.

At the feel of him, a sparkling bouquet of color popped through her, showers of heat jerking through her limbs, all coming together in the center of her to explode in one spray of bliss.

Fireworks, she thought, her brain scrambling in a whirl of sensation.

At first he seemed surprised at what she'd done, and as her common sense returned, she started to pull back from him, keeping her eyes closed so she might hold on to the kiss.

But then she *kept* them closed in dread of what she would see on his face.

My God, had she just surrendered the job she loved for a kiss?

Granted, it'd been a real kiss, yet still…

Bracing herself, she opened her eyes to see the helpless desire returned in his own gaze.

"I'm…" she began to say.

Yet, before she could finish, he slid his hands under her jaw and crushed his mouth to hers, sending jags of white light through her head and blanking out all other thoughts.

There was just him, his lips sucking at hers, devouring as he dug his fingers into her hair.

With something near to a sob, she grasped at his business shirt, wanting more.

As Melanie returned his kiss with a fervor that matched his own, Zane realized at this moment that he needed her more than he had ever needed anything.

Nothing else existed—not the pictures around him, not the walls of the room that seemed to be tumbling down with every passing draw of their lips.

Not the world outside of those walls.

She helped him to escape it all, and for better or worse, that was all he wanted right now. Her borrowed serenity.

Her.

He would think about the consequences later.

"Melanie," he murmured against her lips, saying her name by itself for the first time out loud.

She moaned, sending a shot of lust through him—a feeling he hadn't enjoyed for years.

Not since…

No, he couldn't think about anyone else, not even his ex-wife, as the passion he'd built up all this time threatened to crash.

All he wanted was to tear off that robe he'd bought Melanie the other night, push her back onto the desk and release all the pressure straining to burst within him.

But he forced himself to slow down, to absorb the summer scent of her hair and skin, then let the reality catch up with the fantasies he'd harbored ever since first seeing her.

He tilted her back in his arms, running his lips along her neck, nipping at her warm skin, taking her ear into his mouth and hearing her groan this time.

Her little sounds overwhelmed him, sending him beyond the realms of control he clung to so fiercely, and he yanked at the sash of the robe he'd given to her.

That sense of possession rocked Zane again. She belonged to him—his to take and his to let go when the time came.

But he wasn't going to think about letting go right now….

He slid the silk off to reveal her bare shoulders, then ran his hands over her skin. He'd known how soft it would be, but now he shuddered at the feel of such smoothness under his fingertips.

His libido took over, and he found himself whispering, "I've wanted you so badly."

"Me, too."

His mouth brushed against hers, yet they

hesitated in kissing. Instead, they stayed like this, panting, her breath entering him in a profoundly intimate moment, one he'd never thought to experience again.

Swept away by that, he touched her neck, just as he'd wanted to do last night after shopping, then lightly dragged his fingers downward, over her chest, between her small, firm breasts.

She hauled in a sharp breath, and the blood rushed to his groin, getting him ready for her. And he stayed ready as the tips of her breasts hardened under her nightie.

He traced the outline of one, bringing it to a more stimulated peak. Then he bent to her, touching his tongue to the nub as she lifted one of those gorgeous, long legs and wrapped it around him, urging him even closer.

Close enough so that he was against the center of her, pressing, letting her feel how much he wanted her.

He moved his hips, barely grinding, and she let her head angle back, exposing her throat.

Guiding her backward, he used one arm to clear a spot on his desk, papers and file holders falling to the ground before he laid her on it.

There, where he spent so many of his hours in the blank numbness of business, her hair spread like rays.

Like sunshine, he thought, bending to her breast again and catching her scent, taking more of her into his mouth, dampening the cotton of her nightie while he sucked and worked her with his tongue and teeth.

Now both of her legs were around him, clamping, bringing him to her, where he nudged against her undies.

"Zane," she said, and the sound of his name made him even harder.

He slipped a hand under her nightie, feeling for her panties.

Her hand stopped him, pushing his questing fingers away.

"The door," she said unevenly, "not… locked."

His mind raced around that, but he was too far gone to stop.

Too far gone to even think of what it would be like between him and Melanie after they…

Scooping her into his arms, he walked purposefully to the door, but instead of locking it, he opened it, peering around the hall to see that they were alone, then continuing to his bedroom.

Nothing could stop him. Not even common sense.

His door was already ajar, and he kicked it open the rest of the way, crossing the threshold and then leaning back against the door to shut everything out.

He locked it behind them.

Then he went to the bed, barely realizing that Melanie was gripping his shirt, her face buried against his neck.

As he laid her out on the mattress, she said his name again.

"Zane?"

It was a question, dizzy, uncertain, almost slurred with what he knew she had to be wanting, too.

Yet his name had also been steeped in… feeling. Emotion.

For a torn second, he wondered if they should be doing this—what the price would be for getting it on with the nanny. But then, from somewhere deep inside, a roll of warmth swamped him.

He knew that this woman had been more than just a nanny. She *was* more, and his body had just realized it before any other part of him had.

And it was his body that was in command now. Thankfully, it shut down his brain, and his feelings. It blocked the possibility of emotion from entering this equation—if he even had more to give than the temporary warmth he'd just experienced.

Even so, just looking at her made him want to please her, and he found himself stroking the hair back from her face.

Just one time, he thought. *Just for a moment.*

She closed her eyes, giving into his caress. Then, easing his hands lower, down her chest, her stomach, her hips, he came to her legs.

Her amazing, endless legs that had been driving him wild.

As he'd dreamed about before, he skimmed a thumb over one slim ankle, then upward, exploring every contour until he got to her knee.

She shifted under his touch, asking for more without even a word.

"Dancer's legs," he said, a strange hint of wonder and appreciation in his tone.

A flush settled over her face, and there was something in her eyes…

Before he could decide what it was, the look disappeared, and he couldn't help embracing a sense of relief.

And…disappointment?

No. He couldn't afford disappointment.

"Once you start dancing," she said softly, a quiver to her tone, "it's hard to stop."

No kidding, he thought. He'd been dancing away from a lot of things for years.

He pushed up her nightie, and she squirmed under his hands as he touched places she'd probably never expected him to explore.

Damn, her waist was tiny, her stomach flat, delineated. He ran his thumbs lower, over her hip bones, then down into her panties.

Melanie pressed a hand to her face as he came

back up to rub her belly, up and down, making her shift her hips with his every motion.

He was pulsing, eager for her, and he wasn't going to last much longer, but he couldn't stop watching her face—how she bit her lip, how she arched her neck.

Hell, was he really enough to elicit such emotion from her?

Something deep and low within him responded to the matter of whether feeling truly *wasn't* a part of his life anymore.

As he blanked out that question—he was tired of fighting it, ramming against it—he coaxed Melanie's undies down her legs, then off. He helped her to a sitting position, taking her nightie by the hem and whisking it off her body.

She sat before him, naked and so beautiful that it made his belly tighten.

Steam driving his every move, he started to

unbutton his shirt, but he didn't do it fast enough.

Not for her.

She helped him, fumbling with his buttons.

Her insistence got to him, and while she worked on his shirt, he took care of his trousers and the rest of his clothes, until he was as bare as she was.

Now she was looking at him with such yearning, with such—he had no idea what else was in her gaze, or maybe he just didn't *want* to know—that her attention stoked him to a new level of need.

He had a few condoms in a nightstand, just as he kept one in his wallet—an option, he'd always thought, even though he'd never pursued it. But the expiration date on one in the nightstand was still good. He ripped open a packet and sheathed himself.

She backed toward his headboard, reached

behind her for a pillow and reclined against it.

He moved at the same time, kneeling between her legs, resting himself there.

"Oh," she said as his tip smoothed over her folds. "Inside. Come inside."

He wanted to be there, too, and an inner pressure pounded at him, persuading him to hurry it up.

Taking her by the hips, he slid into her, wallowing in the sensation of her around him, clenching, slick.

And tight, too.

When was the last time she'd been with a man?

His thought process crashed as he thrust inside her again; she took him, grasping his hips, urging him on as they found a rhythm, their own dance.

But this time, instead of dancing away, he

moved toward something—a brightness, a lightness, a feeling that he was floating and leaving the rest of it behind for as long as he could.

They churned, their rhythm quickening as he pushed into her again, again…

"Zane," she said once more, as if his name had turned itself inside out to become something different. Something that only she could see.

She arched under him, rocking, riding the cadence of his thrusts as he disappeared into that light he'd seen.

Blinding, lifting, heating and burning…

It singed him with a blaze of fire, eating at his skin and roaring through him in an explosion that blasted him apart.

She held him through all of it, even as she came soon afterward. Their skin glistened with sweat, their bodies sticking together as if not wanting to separate.

But he *had* separated, he knew as their breath battled, chest to chest.

He'd come undone.

And much to his shock, it hadn't done him in after all.

Chapter Eight

Afterward, they ended up resting next to each other in his bed, and Melanie had no idea what to say or do, except to just lie there and…

And just breathe, she guessed.

She'd never participated in anything close to a one-night stand before, but as the all-encompassing sensual fog dissipated, she wondered if this might be the first instance, because she didn't see how anything could ever develop between her and Zane.

To think, it'd seemed like such a wonderful idea when he had first kissed her. It'd seemed…right. Perfect. As if life had been a rehearsal for everything that had led up to his lips touching hers and making her lose all sense of reason. She'd never felt that way about any man.

Her pulse seemed to stop now.

But just how *did* she feel about Zane Foley?

Did it even matter now that they'd stopped kissing and embracing and…

Her temperature rose during the replay of it, sending her heartbeat back into motion while she pushed her damp hair back from her forehead, then tugged the disheveled covers up and over her body. For some reason, she was suddenly shier than before.

"Well," he said from his side of the bed, where he'd also pulled up the covers, but only to his chest. Just as she'd expected, it was muscled and defined, making her want to put her hands back on it.

"Well," she echoed.

Maybe he would go ahead and fire her, if things would be *this* unimaginably awkward from now on.

It wasn't just that he was the boss, either. Sex wouldn't erase the issues he still had with his first wife. Plus, getting in deeper with him would mean that Melanie would have to come clean about her past, and she couldn't imagine *that* ever going over well.

Just imagine if the press got a hold of that one.

For a man like Zane, who shielded his private life from public scrutiny the best he could, it would be a complication he couldn't afford.

Melanie drew the covers up even more. She didn't intend to tell anyone about where she'd come from or who she'd been. She'd left all that behind, and having to keep her secrets from a lover wouldn't be fair to him at all.

"I sure wasn't planning on this," she said lightly, hoping to introduce the subject, to let him know that she'd lost her head this one time.

As she waited for his response, she thought that this was one of the hardest conversations she'd ever made herself take part in.

He laughed softly. Was it her imagination, or did he seem relieved at how she was laying all the cards out there?

"I wasn't planning on this, either," he said. "Even though I was thinking about it quite a bit."

She tested him with a glance. He'd curled an arm over his head while fixing his eyes on the ceiling. He'd hardly gone back to the cold man she was afraid would return. No, he actually seemed relaxed, with a slight smile on his mouth.

The best man she would ever get, she realized, and she would have to give him up.

Why hadn't she thought this through way back in the study, when they'd still been kissing?

Her libido answered: *because you were swept away, missy.*

"I never believed it would be a smart plan to get this close to my boss," she said. "Any boss."

"Generally, it's not a good idea. Believe it when I tell you that I've never overstepped like this before, either."

"I do believe you." And it made what she had to say all the tougher. "Zane, this has to be just a one-time event. I wouldn't call it a mistake—not remotely—but the last thing Livie needs is a more complex home life to deal with."

She wanted to take it back; then again, she

knew she wouldn't, even if she had to do it all over again.

There was no future at all, she reminded herself. Not if she wanted to outrun what she'd left behind.

"You're right," he said, still watching the ceiling. "One time will have to keep us."

When she rolled to the side to see him better, her heartbeat stumbled. His expression had become almost…vulnerable. More open than she'd ever seen it, even though he was watching the ceiling and not her.

Then something flashed over his expression, altering it enough to make her wary of what had no doubt just gone through his mind.

After another moment, he sat up, the sheet bunched around his hips as he reached toward a nightstand, then opened the drawer to bring out a small box.

When he turned to her again, he'd gone all the way back to normal—the closed-off man she was so used to.

She missed the other guy already, she thought, running a wistful gaze over him. But she had been the one who'd chased him off.

Again, she got after herself for not thinking about the consequences from the very first. Too impulsive. Too taken in by how he owned her when he was near.

But she wouldn't fool herself into thinking that she'd rocked his world so hard that he'd forgotten all about Danielle.

The wounding thought gave her pause.

Was it possible that, by cutting off a relationship before it had really even started with him, she was also protecting herself from the heartbreak she knew would be in store?

Turning that over in her mind, Melanie sat up, too, pressing the covers against her chest.

He was holding a black jewelry box etched with fancy lettering.

"I bought it the other night—and you can bet it wasn't from the McCord franchise." He was so serious. So Zane Foley. "It was a whim, really, along with the wardrobe and the makeover. I was going to put it in your room before you left."

Jewelry…?

Why was he giving this to her right now? she wondered, not taking the box.

A heaviness descended within her as she remembered Livie's dolls. A guilt gift?

Was he pushing her away, too, but in his own manner?

As he cracked open the lid, her hand whipped out to shut it. She wasn't going to take any expensive presents from him, especially after they'd just been together.

"Zane, I can't accept this," she said.

"Melanie…"

Then he seemed to realize the more tawdry aspects of what she might be thinking.

"Oh, damn," he said. "You know, I'm not paying you off or…"

He shook his head and, cursing, got out of bed, as if he needed that distance.

She told herself to avert her eyes as he sought his trousers, then stepped into them, zipping them up. She didn't want to get revved up again, losing her common sense just as she'd done earlier.

But she could still see him in her peripheral vision. Actually, she couldn't bear to *not* see him.

He set the box on the mattress and went for his shirt, putting it on and buttoning it, clearly burying himself in the clothing. "I was waiting out the first fifteen minutes of your personal shopping when I saw what's in that box. It made me think of you. So I bought it before I came to sit with you and Livie in the boutique." His voice got huskier than ever. "It'd look just right on you, Melanie. Just right."

What could she say? In spite of her refusal, he was still offering her this gift, but she wasn't sure exactly why.

Confusion wound through any of the responses she should be making, tangling them so badly that she couldn't pick anything out.

Taking care of his last shirt button, he moved toward the door, but when he got there, he rested his hand on the knob before opening it.

"By the way," he said, "maybe you and Livie can just go ahead and stay a few days more. But it's not because of what…just happened…of course."

"Of course not," she said, finding her voice.

"Because there can't be a second time."

"Right."

He nodded, then left the room, stranding her with whatever was in the box.

Had he been distancing himself in a very Zane Foley way, while brushing her off?

Or maybe, just maybe, had his gift meant more, and he just had no idea how to give it?

With a trembling hand, she pushed the lid up, and the sparkle of a diamond bracelet hit her full force.

Disbelief overcame her first.

Then breathlessness at receiving such a present.

How many times had she dreamed of a better life? Not necessarily *this* much better, but for a girl whose biggest encounter with decadence came in the form of rhinestones, this was flabbergasting.

But didn't he realize that he'd already made her feel on top of the world without any gifts?

That just being with him gave her a glow that no diamond could compete with?

She wished he were still in here so she could thank him, yet reiterate that she couldn't accept such a present from him or anyone else.

But if this really was a heartfelt offering, wouldn't it be bad form to give it back?

Would it be like a refusal of *him?*

Since it was likely that the only way Zane even knew how to express himself was through dolls and shopping sprees and jewelry, she wasn't sure what to do.

But he'd asked her and Livie to stay longer, and maybe she could figure it out with the extra time.

Yet, even if she did accept the jewelry, or the cosmetics and spiffy clothes she'd been given at the makeover, she knew nothing could change who she'd been.

It wouldn't make her suitable for Zane Foley, even if in her heart, she knew there couldn't be any other man who fit her so perfectly.

Days passed, and Zane found that it was easier than usual to spend time with Livie after his hours at the office. As a matter of fact, his daughter had ended up lingering for more than just a few days; one had stretched into another, and it'd gotten to the point where Zane didn't even mention their staying longer anymore. It just happened on its own.

He'd even started to think that, when it finally came time for them to go, it wouldn't be easy.

Then again, neither was being around Melanie.

She hadn't been wearing the bracelet he gave her, and she told him once, when they were alone, that she appreciated the bracelet, but that donning it right now wasn't appropriate.

He wasn't sure what that meant, but then again, they hadn't been alone long enough for her to explain. In fact, they'd only been together that one night, yet he couldn't forget how he had gone from pure happiness at making love to her, to something else entirely.

And that was why he'd given her the bracelet, he thought a few days later, as he, Melanie and Livie took a stroll through the neighborhood while the sun dipped its way to dusk. He wanted to thank her for giving him even an hour of forgetfulness and then letting him off the hook as far as a commitment went because, honestly, he hadn't wanted one.

Yes, he had flashes of wondering what it might be like as he'd joined with her, moved within her, but when he'd come back to earth, he knew it couldn't last. He wasn't very good at relating such matters with words, although he had meant the gift with all of his soul.

He'd wanted to see her eyes shine, wanted to show her that she was worth diamonds and jewelry.

Unfortunately, she had misinterpreted his gesture at first, but now he wouldn't be surprised if she'd had it all figured out: a diamond bracelet had been the best he could do in a world where he couldn't allow his heart to be touched by anyone, ever again.

Now, as Livie wandered ahead with Melanie to a walking trail that wound through pine trees, he took what he could from the time he would have left with his daughter and her nanny.

It would have to be enough.

Livie scampered up ahead to investigate some stones, leaving Melanie between her and Zane; he slowed down, hanging back, just watching, not getting too close.

Maybe that was because of the anniversary, though, he thought. Danielle's death.

Only two days away.

He leaned against an oak tree, but the bark felt rough against his business shirt. With every hour that counted down to Danielle's day, he felt that much more abraded.

"Ms. Grandy?" his daughter said as she used her long summer shirt to hold a few stones.

"Yes, Livie?" Melanie peered over the girl's shoulder, seeing what she was doing.

"Don't look, okay?" His daughter smiled, her eyes lively as she hid the stones from her nanny. "I want to make a castle for you."

Zane's heart swelled at Livie's apparent joy. They had Melanie to thank for bringing them so far along.

Yet he knew that there were still miles and miles to go.

Playfully, Melanie walked away from Livie, her hands up as if in surrender. And as she came near him, he thought how there were also miles and miles that stayed between him and so many things.

He tried to strengthen himself against the temptation of her, concentrating instead on how the trees smelled in the warm air, how a breeze rustled the pine needles. But nature was hardly enough to keep him from thinking about her body, naked and lean, perfectly formed and so alive under his hands as he'd slid them along her.

Quivers vibrated in his belly, inviting the blood to rush downward.

He resisted, though, still musing about those trees.

Not that it did any good.

She smiled almost shyly at him as she approached, and Zane did the same. But when she got about five feet away, she stayed there, just as if there was a bubble of tension between them, and it was filled with every memory of a caress, of what they'd said to each other, of how she'd touched him....

"Thanks for coming with us," she said, clearly opting for a neutral topic that wouldn't shatter the bubble.

"Livie seemed excited about the prospect."

"She insisted on waiting until you got home."

This was prattle, and it unnerved Zane.

He looked too long at Melanie's inquiring gaze, and he could tell that there was something else she wanted to talk about.

Should he ask?

Dammit, there was no way he could tolerate himself if he continued to practice avoidance, as he had before Melanie had come along. Before his relationship with Livie had started to improve.

"What's on your mind?" he asked.

She gave him a "nothing big" glance, and he motioned for her to come out with it.

"You're not going to want to hear," she said.

"I'm sure I'll hear it anyway at some point."

He laughed a little, and she did, too. Maybe sleeping together had done something for their working relationship.

As well as for *him*.

Trying not to put too much stock in that, he said, "Why don't you just go ahead and tell me, then I'll decide if I should've heard it or not."

"Okay then. It's about…" She folded her hands in front of her, nervous tell. "Livie's mom."

Zane felt punched, but he didn't want to show it.

He wouldn't be able to duck any questions from Livie, either, because it was only natural for his daughter to be asking more of them, now that she was getting comfortable around him.

Melanie continued, keeping those few feet away from him, and he thought that it might be because of the subject, not just him.

"Livie was asking again about things Danielle enjoyed," she said. "I think she wants to imagine what it might've been like to have a fun day with her mom."

He might as well give up a tidbit, so they would be satisfied for the time being. "Danielle was a homebody most of the time. She would've liked teaching Livie to make cookies or play the piano. But when she went out, she might've taken her to a park over near White Rock Lake, where there was this little place called the Wishing Bridge. She would've brought a picnic, just like you do with Livie."

He hadn't meant to compare Melanie and Danielle; it'd just come out, and the aftermath was like recovering from another slam from an invisible fist.

She must've felt it, too, because her face reddened.

He wished he could brush the embarrassment away, make her feel better. He even wished he could tell her that, out of everyone in this world, she was the closest Livie had ever come to a mom.

But he didn't. Neither Livie nor he could survive another Danielle.

"Six years ago Saturday," he said instead, creating more distance, "Danielle died."

Melanie blinked, as if taken off balance.

Why had he said it? Because he needed to keep that bubble intact between them?

She kept her hands folded in front of her. "Livie doesn't know about this anniversary," she said.

"No. I never wanted to put that on her."

"Zane…" Cutting herself off, she glanced at Livie, who was choosing more rocks to put into the scoop of her shirt. Then she snagged his gaze. "Zane."

Her voice was softer, with a hint of emotion he wished he could connect to again, yet, with Danielle's name filling that bubble with so much, there was no chance.

Melanie seemed to realize that as she went on. The sadness in her usually sparkling eyes told him so.

"Don't you think," she said, "that Livie might be getting old enough to take a day when she can remember her mom? Maybe not this anniversary—not yet—but even on Danielle's birthday, which I know you don't acknowledge, either?"

"Stop it, Melanie." His voice was harsh, guarded.

"Zane, please, I'd like to take her to that park on Saturday, to that bridge, where she can be with her mom, and if she doesn't know why, that's okay. Can't you see how badly she wants to be with Danielle, even if it's only in a place her mom *used* to love?"

Rage—not at Melanie, necessarily, but at everything else—blinded him.

"Can't *you* see that she's better off without Danielle?" he asked in a crushed whisper.

She got that fighting look about her again—that chin-up, David-against-Goliath strength.

"No one is better off without their family," she said quietly. "Take it from me. You're doing her no favors by never talking about her mother at all."

Zane's anger filtered out everything but the "take it from me" part.

It occurred to him that Melanie didn't talk about her family much at all. Sure, she had done so during her second interview when he'd pressed the issue, but even back then he'd noticed a cautiousness that came along with her answers.

She seemed to realize it, too, veering back to the subject at hand.

"Please, Zane," she said.

He was still simmering, but underneath it all, he had to admit she was right.

He hadn't merely been withholding *himself* from his daughter, he'd been keeping her mom away from her, too.

But what would it do to Livie when she found out just how bad off Danielle had been? What would she do when she realized that her mom's worst days had come after childbirth, which had seemed to drive her into a dark place—for which she'd taken stronger mood stabilizers—a place that had consumed her when she'd become too confident about her "wellness" and secretly gone off the meds that had been prescribed when she'd gotten worse?

The more you keep from Livie, he thought, *the more she's going to want to know.*

Yet, his daughter didn't have to know everything, did she? Not even when she was older. But for now, maybe it really would benefit her to get acquainted with the woman Zane had loved.

He warmed slightly to the idea—as much as he could.

This trip to the bridge didn't even have to include *him.* In fact, it wouldn't, because he would have no part of a day that marked the discovery of his wife in the bathroom, lethal pills spilled over the tile next to her slumped body.

He made himself forget.

"I won't go with you," he said, "but you can take Livie to that bridge Saturday."

Melanie nodded, as if knowing he didn't have it in him to change all that much.

"Thank you," she said. "And if you decide that you want to come, too, we'll be there."

We'll be there.

He didn't answer, but then again, he didn't have to, as Livie called to Melanie to come see the stone castle she'd built. A structure that would probably crumble all too soon.

Melanie didn't prepare for Danielle's anniversary until that Saturday morning, when the sun didn't shine as brightly as usual.

It was only after she'd garbed Livie in a pretty sundress, combed out her wavy hair for a pair of pigtails and driven her to Crane Park, that she told the child just where they were going—but not why.

Yet, even then, she hardly trusted her voice to hold itself together as they walked over the grass toward a quaint wooden bridge etched with dove carvings.

There were plenty of things Melanie wouldn't be telling Livie: that her father had refused to be here with them on this important day; that she suspected he would never move forward, never mend himself so he could…

Melanie swallowed and clutched Livie's hand.

She'd been having wasted dreams that maybe he would mend enough that they *could* have a future together, no matter what she'd determined on the night they had been intimate. But it was only wishful thinking, because even then, that wouldn't get rid of her own reasons for staying away from him.

Yet, if she wanted to stay away, why had she let out a piece of her past the other day, when she mentioned how everyone needed family? She'd never meant for him to know how she felt about the people she'd left behind in

Oklahoma, but when she had that slip of the tongue, she'd hoped that she'd given Zane enough room to share his burdens with her, too.

Apparently, he hadn't wanted to, so here she was, with his daughter, taking up where he'd left off.

Livie was watching Melanie with those big eyes, just as if she knew something was different about today, and Melanie squeezed her hand as they came to the foot of the bridge. Around them, only a few other people meandered through the park, and the birds only gave little chirps, as if they were just as subdued as Melanie was feeling. Even the stream seemed to lack some burble.

"You like this bridge?" Melanie asked, her throat acting as if it was closing in on itself.

Livie nodded. "It looks like Snow White."

Yes, Melanie could see some Seven

Dwarves in the structure, just as she could see Danielle in Livie.

She brought the little girl onto the planking, then to the center, where they sat just above the water.

"I heard," she said, "that this was one of your mom's favorite places."

Livie's eyes lit up. "My mom?"

"Yes."

The little girl smiled so wide that Melanie's gaze blurred, hot and watery. Years from now, she would finally understand why Melanie had brought her to the park today, and hopefully it would, among other things, show Livie how much her nanny had loved her.

The child placed her hand on the carved rail above them, where a wooden flower bloomed. "I was a baby, but I think I remember her."

A tear wiggled down Melanie's cheek, but she subtly dried it with a finger. "Really?"

"She sang me songs. Monty told me, and he sang one when he had to drive me to the doctor for…"

"A checkup?" Melanie touched Livie's back. So small, so frail right now. So in need of someone. "Which song?"

Livie looked into the water, as if trying to recall. Then she began to hum a sad tune. A lullaby that stopped after a few notes.

"That's all I know," the child said, softer now.

Another tear ran down Melanie's face as she hugged Livie to her. She wished Zane was here to tell his daughter which song it had been, maybe even to hum the rest of it for her.

"She smelled like oranges, too," the child said, leaning against Melanie now. "Monty said that, but I don't really remember."

"Oranges…" Melanie could barely get the words out, so she cleared her throat, waited a moment, then tried again, even though she succeeded in only whispering. "That was no doubt her perfume. Orange blossom."

Livie turned her face up to Melanie, still smiling, and she knew that she'd done good in bringing her here.

Done real good, even for a woman who'd grown up on the wrong side of the tracks.

Then Livie's gaze settled on something behind Melanie.

Her blood expanded in her veins when a voice followed.

"Orange blossom," Zane Foley said, his tone that of a man who was living a certain hell by just being here. "I remember that perfume, Livie."

His daughter sprang up to greet her dad as Melanie turned around, tears destroying her vision until she wiped them away, allowing her to see him desperately embracing Livie, his eyes closed tightly. He was holding Danielle's urn in one hand, his little girl in the other.

He came, Melanie thought.

And when he and Livie paused to look at each other, Melanie could see how red his eyes were, how quietly devastated he'd been all these years, while trying to keep it from everyone else.

She stood, thinking she should leave him and Livie alone.

But then he spoke.

"Melanie?" he asked, his voice ragged, and she could see that he was asking her to join them.

Without hesitation, she went to them, the tears coming freely as they both drew her into their circle.

Melanie held on to them. Lord help her, she hadn't just fallen for Livie.

She'd fallen for all of them.

Chapter Nine

The morning had ended up being a catharsis for Zane.

Ever since Melanie had asked to take Livie to the bridge, he'd wrestled with his conscience—and his emotions. By the time Saturday had arrived, he'd been mentally beating himself up with such frequency that he was exhausted.

While he sat in his study, listening to the stirrings of Melanie and Livie departing for

Crane Park, the house had seemed to suck in on him, making it hard to breathe.

It only got worse after they were gone, with the clock in the foyer ticking away, providing the only sound.

Buried alive, he kept thinking, and each *thunk* of the clock's hand was like another shovel full of dirt against him.

This would be the rest of his life. In so many ways, he was just as absent as Danielle was.

But as the chime marked the hour, he realized that he'd felt a hell of a lot more present since Melanie and Livie had come around.

So why was he now accepting this never-ending descent into nothing?

Why was he forcing himself to live like this?

Before he could change his mind, he'd taken Danielle's ashes out of that chest, unburying the urn for all intents and purposes, then went to the park, at first hanging back from Melanie and Livie, then approaching them step by slow step.

After they'd welcomed him, he felt free for the first time in years, as if he'd escaped the fate he'd sentenced himself to. And as the trio of them had embraced upon that bridge, the truth became so very clear.

He didn't want Livie and Melanie to go anywhere.

Zane wasn't sure what he should do about that, or even if he could manage to never let them down again, but he wanted to keep them near.

Afterward, they'd spent another hour at the park, spreading Danielle's ashes at both entrances to the bridge. It had seemed so symbolic. A bridge, spanning from one side to another. A crossing.

Then, while Melanie left them alone so he could walk with Livie, he'd told his daughter about Danielle's good days, although he took care to hint that her mother hadn't been perfect. But she'd loved her daughter in her own way, even if she had died long before her time.

He would tell Livie more as the years went by, he thought, but for now, she seemed content to have her father finally talking.

When they arrived back at the townhouse, Melanie left father and daughter alone again, and they went through boxed pictures of Danielle that Zane had pushed to the back of the garage. He chalked up their nanny's absence to her ongoing respect of what he and Livie needed to clear with each other; but once, when Melanie had looked in on them to ask if they were hungry, he saw a cloudiness in her gaze, and that had tweaked something within Zane.

After she'd left the room, he thought about just how to thank her for all her guidance and softhearted patience. For everything she'd done for him and his family.

So he'd gone about it in the only way he could manage.

Which brought him to the present, and his newest gift, which was steered into the driveway by Monty. Zane thought that Melanie couldn't possibly refuse *this* gesture. Surely she would see, this time, that he wasn't thanking her with a bracelet for needing him or trying to win her over with a night in a posh department store.

Monty opened the door of the new silver Mercedes S Class and stretched out his long legs.

"Drives like butter!" he said, as happy as any man behind the wheel of a dream machine.

Early this morning, after telling Zane that he wanted to give this baby a spin before it fell out of his hands, Monty had been picked up by a sales representative. And, now, as Livie darted out of the front door and into the driveway, Zane fully recognized the lure of this shiny present.

It was the very best he could offer.

"Mr. Monty!" the little girl said, running to the driver, who ruffled her hair in greeting. "I like your car. Can I drive it?"

"Sure, but I should let you know this belongs to Ms. Grandy, not me."

"Oh, she's *lucky.*"

Monty grinned at Zane, entirely skipping over the need to explain the subtleties of Melanie's new car. Hell, Zane hadn't bothered to tell the driver anything except that Melanie was receiving a bonus for a job well done, and it was a believable story, since Zane often doled out high-priced rewards to other employees.

"Hop right in," Monty said to Livie, as he held open the driver's door for her.

She climbed inside, and Zane knew his daughter wouldn't be burning rubber out of the driveway; Monty occasionally allowed her to play in the cars while he watched to see that she didn't cause any mischief.

As a shiver waved over his skin, Zane turned to find Melanie coming out of the townhouse, too. Even while she remained at the top of the driveway, the impact of her presence scrambled him to the point of jagged confusion.

Gratefulness. Tenderness.

Guilt?

He wasn't sure exactly what he felt, but whatever the emotion, he seemed to exude it, because he could've sworn that she had momentarily held her breath at the sight of him, just as affected as he was by merely being in the same area.

He swept his hand toward the car. "Your coach awaits."

"*My* coach?"

With a doubtful expression, she folded her hands in front of her in that anxious gesture, and he had the feeling that she was beginning to understand what he was up to.

If only he knew, too.

"It's yours," he said.

From the side of the car, where Monty was watching over Livie, the driver added, "A bonus! We all get 'em, Ms. Grandy, so don't look like the rug's going to be pulled out from under you."

As Melanie took that in, Zane could see her shoulders slump a bit. Why? Did she *want* to be *more* than only an employee?

Yet, he already knew that she was much more than someone he gave a paycheck to, or even someone who'd eased his pain yesterday, as well as on that one, earth-moving night they'd been together.

She was so much more.

He just didn't know what, exactly.

Zane stepped toward the car. "What do you say we take this on the road?"

"Mr. Foley..." she said, using his formal name around the others.

He stopped her before she could tell him that she wouldn't accept this, just as she had done with the bracelet.

"'No' isn't an option," he said.

Monty was already ushering Livie out of the front seat.

"I *love* your car," the girl said to her nanny as the driver shepherded Livie toward the house.

Melanie only smiled as Monty indicated he would look after the child while Melanie enjoyed a test drive. Then he got Livie through the front door.

Zane started to go around to the passenger's side. "Let's go."

"Where? Back to the dealership?"

"Come on, Melanie." Zane opened the door and leaned on the top of it. "Indulge me?"

She sighed and he took that as a good sign, getting in and closing his door.

When she slid in, too, she didn't start the engine. "You know what I'm going to say, right? Thank you but—"

"It's the same thing you said about the bracelet. And, as I recall, you never did give that back to me, so I assume it's accepted."

She kept looking at him as if she were about to hand him a much more detailed answer that he probably wouldn't want to hear.

A refusal, he realized, and it chipped away at him, revealing a raw side that he thought he'd gotten control of after getting home from Danielle's bridge yesterday. It was a part of him that would come out next anniversary, then the next, and that was all he could allow.

Then again, Melanie hadn't run away at any point. Hadn't she seen the worst of him already?

What was he afraid of, then?

"Do you know just how much you've meant to me and Livie?" he asked quietly, taking a chance, breaking his own rules and hoping she wouldn't get out of this car and leave him.

She touched the steering wheel, longing written all over her face. Yet somehow, he got the feeling that she wasn't craving a car.

"I know how much you two appreciate me," she said. "So you don't have to give me things to prove it."

"I only want to—"

She faced him. "Did you love her so much that you can't bring yourself to dig all the way out of it, Zane?"

Melanie was referring to Danielle, and for

a decimated heartbeat, he didn't know how to answer.

"I'm sorry," she said, raising her hands from the wheel. "I can't believe I just asked. I shouldn't have."

He gently grabbed her wrist before she could go anywhere, and she stayed, watching him with those eyes—that clear gaze hazed with gathering clouds.

"I did love her," he found himself saying, even though there was still a part of him that warned against it. "I loved her so much that, when she died, it killed most of me, too."

Zane let go of her wrist. He was numb again, hardly believing the words that had come out of his mouth.

Just shut up, he told himself. *Stop now.*

But he didn't, because he was sick of holding it in, and yesterday, when some of it had been released, he'd actually felt like a new man.

Thing was, he didn't know who that man was or where he was going—or even how to get there.

The image of that bridge entered his mind, but it faded all too quickly.

"I'm not even sure," he heard himself saying, "that I'll ever really be there for anyone else. But you've come the closest to showing me the way, Melanie. You…" He almost didn't say it, but it came out nonetheless. "You were the first woman I've been with since Danielle."

God, he sounded like a monk—but hadn't he shut himself away just as thoroughly?

Gaze softening, Melanie opened her mouth to respond, but he got there first.

"I know, I know—withdrawn in the extreme. But I wouldn't have been good for anyone. You could probably testify to that. And I only wanted to give you back a little of what you gave to me, whether it was with a car or a bracelet…."

"I understand."

She came into vivid focus now—Melanie, a constant that was so much warmer than the work that had sustained him before.

But she was also more volatile. Work would always be there for him, no matter how he treated it; yet, she would take so much more care, and there was no guarantee that she would stay.

She laid her hand on his arm, and those shivers of desire returned to thrust at him deep inside.

"I just wish I could take all that pain from you, Zane," she said.

When he looked into her eyes, he saw that she truly would if she could.

He shook his head. "You don't want to know everything."

"Why? Because I might break under all of it?"

Melanie rubbed her thumb back and forth over his arm, not in a seductive way, but in a manner that reminded him of a soft breeze blowing over cushioning grass.

She continued. "I did some research into bipolar disorder, just to try and understand that, too. I didn't get past a lot of the technical information, though."

Right. The definitions of BP—*abnormal alterations in moods, energy and the ability to function*—were easy to learn.

The rest wasn't easy.

But she'd tried, Zane thought, and the proof of it touched him.

"All along," he said, "Danielle would have episodes, both manic and depressive. She had blamed me and her family before for her troubles. She even had to be hospitalized a couple of times before the pregnancy. But after Livie was born, she just…" He blew out a breath. "She started saying that she was a burden—that she'd brought me too much trouble, even though I did everything I could to show her that I loved her and Livie. That's when she went on stronger mood stabilizers, and they seemed to work."

"Until she went off of those?" Melanie added.

Zane nodded, not wanting to talk about the suicide itself. Not yet. Maybe not ever, because it cut too close, even after a six-year anniversary.

"And Livie?" Melanie asked, sounding anxious. "I heard that children of parents with the illness are more likely to have the disorder."

"She's visited doctors, and they believe she's normal."

Yet his daughter had been through so much that Zane wasn't sure what normal really was.

He added, "But she'll keep seeing them. I want to be sure."

"Right." Melanie slid her hand down his arm. "You did everything you could do, and you're doing the same thing now, Zane. So stop hounding yourself."

Melanie was holding his arm, as if trying to transfer strength, and oddly enough, he actually felt it.

Or did he just want it so badly that he was imagining it?

"You don't have to tell me that you're afraid Livie's going to be like Danielle," she said. "You've set yourself back from her, just in case it ever does happen again. But, good heavens, Zane, there's no guarantee there'll be a next time. You can't live in anticipation of it."

"I wish I could believe that."

As if making him want to believe, Melanie brought her fingers to his temple, where she brushed the hair away from his face.

He allowed the wash of comfort to ease through him. She was the only one who could make him think that there were wonderful possibilities ahead, and he wished he could accept everything she had to offer.

But what else was he going to do? Keep going backward instead of moving on?

When he didn't react right away, Melanie stopped touching him, starting up the car instead and then backing it out of the driveway for the spin he wanted her to take.

And although her acceptance of this latest present gratified him, it was the afterburn of her fingers on his skin that kept him going.

Move on, he thought as he gave himself over to the idea.

Because if he was ever going to do it, the time was now.

* * *

Throughout the drive around the neighborhood, Melanie finally accepted that this car was hers, and she acknowledged the magnitude of this bonus that Zane had given her.

But she was even more overwhelmed by his other gift: the truth about Danielle.

"I loved her so much that, when she died, it killed most of me, too," he'd said, and the confession still seared her, like a brand that would always be there.

She hadn't expected him to forget about Danielle anytime soon, but when he said that…?

The words still lingered, becoming darker with the reality of how difficult it would be to love a man with such ghosts.

Then again, she was used to difficult, wasn't she? Couldn't she be up to the challenge of telling him that she loved him enough to work with his demons?

As she aimed the car back into the driveway of his townhouse, she knew she would never even get the chance, because that would mean coming clean about her own truths.

But, dammit, she was doing so well as this new person—a *decent* person—who'd helped Zane and Livie. Couldn't she continue as Melanie the nanny?

Couldn't she avoid beating him back down again by slamming him with the truth of her own past?

She'd gotten in too deep; yet, she wanted to be here with all her heart and soul. The new Melanie was good for him and his daughter.

He used a remote to open the door of the stand-alone garage, and she parked next to his personal ride—a black Jaguar that he didn't drive much. Since he'd already done away with the vehicle she'd been driving before, that left room for her.

For Melanie Grandy, the woman who would do almost anything for him.

Almost.

While she got out, he shut the garage behind them, and she began to walk toward the regular door, which stood opposite the townhouse.

But then he slid his arm around her waist, turning her to face him and keeping her from going anywhere.

The contact made her circuits go haywire.

"Zane, what are you—"

He stopped her with a soft kiss, and she held on to his arms, leaning into him, helpless.

Every nerve ending seemed to short out, sparking her skin as he kept his mouth against hers while she talked.

"What are you doing?" she murmured.

"Kissing you."

Oh, not a good idea, she thought as she went pliant under another kiss—soft, tender. She was going to be a pool of nothing in another second.

When he came up from her, he smiled, and there was something like hope in his eyes.

And that hope kept her in his arms, because she hadn't seen such a thing in him before; she knew that she helped to put it there.

"There's no need to remind me that we said we wouldn't have anything more to do with each other." He pressed his mouth against her ear. "But dammit, Melanie."

No, dammit, *Zane.*

Their discussion in the car had been an opportunity to relieve himself of feelings he'd been containing for a long time. And when Melanie had touched him, comforting him, he'd probably seen that as…

Well, she wasn't sure. She hadn't meant to escalate anything, only to make him feel better.

But now, as he ran his lips around her ear, heating it with his tight breaths, she thought that his body was taking the place of the other gifts. He was expressing his thanks in a much more physical way that she wasn't able to resist.

Yet she had to.

"We should stop," she said, knowing where their kiss had ended up the last time.

Hardly stopping, he pressed his lips against her jaw, her cheek, working his way back toward her mouth.

As she nearly swayed under the flow of feeling, she recalled when he'd told her about being with no other women since Danielle. She'd been shocked, but it also made such sense. Zane had been closed; but now, with her, he could release everything he'd kept back.

She'd been the one who brought that out in him. The new Melanie Grandy.

Didn't that count for anything at all? Shouldn't that allow her to enjoy his kisses, his…

His *everything?*

Guilt still reared up and made her draw away, even if her body hated her for it.

But he kept a hold on her hands. "I keep thinking about the first time with us. I can't forget."

"Same here, but…"

Lord, there were too many "but"s to bring up.

"Hey. You just got shyer on me. You do that sometimes." He tipped a finger under her chin. "What're you all about, Melanie Grandy?"

A flush shot through her, from neck to chest. He wanted her to talk about herself, didn't he?

Oh, no.

"You're the one who interviewed me," she said. "You've already got the answers."

"Hardly."

As much as she wanted to stay away from the subject altogether, she knew that Zane wouldn't be happy until she offered him a little bit of her.

Yet, what would she do when he wanted more?

She couldn't think about that right now. "I've always been a tad shy, even though you might not know it."

"No, your bashful streak is there, all right."

He skimmed his fingers over her cheek, and she almost lost it.

"I was just never the dating-around type, I suppose." She shrugged, willing to tell him this much, but intending to skip over the section of her past where she went on a few innocent dates, all right, but she'd done it mainly to avoid going home to that double-wide trailer. "There're only a couple guys of note. One in high school—puppy love."

"Was he your first?" Zane asked, looking amused.

She was glad to see that this conversation at least cheered him, taking him far away from the memory of Danielle.

"Yes," she said. "I thought he was *it* for me. But it didn't turn out that way after he went off to college."

"I was with a few girls in high school before Danielle came along. Then…"

The shadows started coming back, and she fought to fend them off.

"My second 'big thing' was a guy in Vegas," she offered.

And…yes: success.

The shadows fell away from his gaze and

she smiled, encouraging a growing light in his eyes again; it caused that love she'd named only yesterday to swell up through her chest, making her feel elevated.

He tucked a strand of her hair behind her ear. "What about that guy in Vegas?"

"He wasn't the one."

The words just hung there, as filmy and sticky as a web to avoid.

But he seemed to get caught in it, maybe even translating her message as it was meant to be: *Zane* was the one—a man like no other. Yet there was no way she could say it out loud.

With a passion that made her pull in a breath, he held her against him, reaching over to lock the garage door at the same time.

Oh, no.

Oh, yes.

She wanted this more than anything, and once again she was starting to forget all the reasons they'd stayed apart.

"You know about the Fourth of July charity event at Tall Oaks?" he asked, as he inched her shirt out of the shorts she was wearing.

She nodded, unable to do anything else.

"I'd be happy if you'd be by my side to help me see to the details," he said, running his thumbs up and down her stomach.

Although she could hardly think at all, she thought he might be asking her to be a hostess.

Was he?

Did he want her to be out on the lawn at Tall Oaks with him and all his friends and family?

Half of her panicked, but the other half was encompassed and embraced in a way she'd never felt before.

"Be there with me," he said, moving in back

of her, one hand staying on her belly. "And be with me *here,* Melanie. I'm ready for it. I swear."

But was *she* ready?

As his hands traveled up to cup her breasts she gasped, leaning back against him.

Such a bad idea, she kept thinking, but only because she was still hiding so much of herself from him. Yet, if he only knew who she'd been, he would drop her.

And from this height, she wouldn't be able to stand the fall.

He kissed her neck, sending lightning bolts of heat through her, and soon he had her clothes off, exploring every inch of her body.

His, she thought. She was all his.

She turned around, helping him with his clothing, too, as he backed her toward the backseat of her new car.

Suddenly, she felt like a teenager—giddy

and fresh and a little afraid of what was going to come next.

But it was that newness that made her think that this *could* work—that they were both starting out together in a different direction. That they were going to try their damnedest to turn everything around and be the family they'd both been lacking.

As he eased her down to the backseat—the upholstery leather soft, smooth and creamy—he used his fingers to prepare her, even though it didn't take long, because she was already there.

And after he got a condom out of his wallet, slid it on and then slipped into Melanie, she cried out, softly, joyfully.

Whole. This is what it's like to have every missing part come together.

All those parts swirled, whirling up and blasting through everything in their path, as the two of them moved together, blazing, zooming, driving…

Delivering her with a crash to that new place she'd been hoping for.

Chapter Ten

As the Fourth of July approached, Melanie, Zane and Livie returned to Tall Oaks to see to the last of the party details for the annual Dallas Children's Hospital charity event.

Although Melanie claimed the guest room again, she didn't stay there at night.

Rather, she spent every hour possible with Zane, just as they'd been doing ever since that day when they'd decided they couldn't stand to be apart.

Everything else had fallen into place after their reunion: Livie continued to grow closer to her nanny, and there were even times when Melanie felt more like a mother to her than a caretaker. And unlike her "previous life," Melanie now felt financially secure—or actually, she felt *secure,* plain and simple.

It all had to do with the fact that she was in love with Zane, though neither of them had said it yet.

But she felt it, and that was a good enough start.

On the afternoon of the charity event, Melanie flitted around anxiously, checking with Mrs. Howe regarding how they would handle people who wished to tour the Victorian mansion, and putting her head together with Scott, the cook, about catering arrangements, then going over logistics one more time with Zane's assistant, Cindy.

Initially, Melanie had approached the situation with an acute awareness that nannies didn't usually take over like this. But if the others thought it odd, no one said anything, maybe because they saw that Melanie only wanted to be as helpful as she could.

With everything in place now, she calmed herself by giving one last inspection to the house and, finally, the sitting room: the pastoral oil landscape on the wall, the organ in the corner, the bars of Sassy, the canary's, cage.

Maybe the bird had picked up on the change in the household, because it was singing at the moment, tweeting away and making Melanie laugh.

She glanced around the new and improved interior of Tall Oaks. There hadn't been enough time to restore the paintings on the ceilings, but the rest of the place gleamed more than it had before.

Danielle would've been proud, Melanie thought, feeling a connection with the woman, although Zane had told her that his first wife had only used Tall Oaks on some weekends. He'd sold their main house following her death.

The notion smoothed out Melanie's smile until Livie bounded into the room.

The little girl was already set to celebrate, and she was so cute, with that light dusting of freckles over the bridge of her nose and the dimples she'd started to show more and more, that she could've melted the polar ice cap. She wore a prim pink sundress, her dark, wavy hair in a low, understated ponytail. Her outfit matched the occasion—a fancy Texas cocktail party, complete with steaks and all the trimmings.

"I smell like sunscreen," Livie said.

"You'll need it out there." Melanie wiped at

a streak of white on Livie's cheek. "Even if we're going to be in those big tents most of the time, I want to make sure you're covered."

"And when are you getting ready? I can't wait to see you. You'll be the prettiest lady there."

Although Melanie thanked Livie, she highly doubted it. The cream of the social crop would be present today, and her stomach kept turning at the thought of mingling with them and having them realize that, truthfully, she didn't really belong.

Had she only been fooling herself with Zane, while they'd stayed pretty much to themselves in Dallas? Would any of these new, genuinely elegant people see an area of her own personality that hadn't been polished enough?

Would they know where she'd really come from?

But when Livie took her nanny's hand, leading her toward the stairs and her room to get ready, Melanie thought that where she'd been didn't matter as much as where she was now.

When they came to the upstairs guest room, Melanie said, "Did you put sunscreen on your arms, Livie?"

The child wrinkled her nose and marched off toward the bathroom where the lotion was kept. "Aw, Ms. Grandy."

"Aw, Livie. Please do it. I'll be checking."

She grinned at the girl, then closed her door just after Livie returned the smile and marched down the hallway.

That left Melanie alone with the blue cocktail dress that hung from a hook inside the closet door. It was one of the pieces Zane had purchased for her during the makeover, and there'd been no occasion to wear it since.

Yet, now Melanie sloughed off her regular-girl shirt and shorts, going to the dress, slipping into it. Then she fixed her hair as the stylist had taught her during the makeover, applying cosmetics just as carefully, too.

As she stood in front of a full-length mirror, going over herself as she'd gone over the final arrangements for the party itself, she heard her door open, then close.

Zane eased up behind her, holding her to him, and her body went crazy with heat.

"I'm not going to be able to take my eyes off you," he whispered into her ear.

The sight of him snuggling with her in the mirror made her weak in the knees. "You'd best try, Zane. Among the other guests, you've got a hoard of business associates who paid a thousand dollars per ticket."

"Forget business."

He kissed her in the sensitive place between her ear and neck, and although she trembled, she knew he wouldn't forget business. He'd taken some unprecedented days away from the Dallas office, but he still brought contracts and other stacks of paper with him.

It was almost as if work was the one thing he couldn't leave behind at all.

Yet, he would come out of that, she thought, optimistic until the end. She was going to make sure he saw that his workaholic nature was to blame for his hiding away from Livie, and that he would never go back there again.

It was still something to work on, but they would succeed, just as she'd always tried so hard to do herself.

He was watching her in the mirror, and she reached back to brush her fingertips over his cheek.

"I wish we had more time before we have to go down to the party," she said.

"Same here." He kissed her jaw. "You're perfect, so perfect, Melanie, but I can't help thinking that there's just one thing missing."

He smiled against her neck. "Where's that bracelet?"

She'd accepted all his gifts by now, and she went to fetch this one from a drawer, taking it out of the box and bringing it back to him so he could help her with the clasp.

In front of the mirror, he took the bracelet, coaxed the diamonds around her wrist and, oh, dear Lord, the lovely weight of them shimmered, just like the future she'd always aimed for.

"And…" he said, taking another small box out of his suit pocket.

He lifted the lid to reveal a pair of diamond earrings.

She should have been over the moon for them, and she smiled as if she were, but she couldn't stop thinking about how he was still offering these gifts, when all she wanted was to hear a simple "I love you" instead.

Melanie held back a sigh. She wouldn't push it, because when that day came, she would come face-to-face with having to tell him about her past. She didn't see how any kind of life-long relationship could survive without that happening.

She would have to make a choice—one she was struggling with even now—because the last thing she wanted was to lose him.

Which, thanks to her, might happen either way.

As fear clutched at Melanie, Zane turned her toward the mirror, clipping the earrings on her lobes, then resting his hands on her shoulders.

"How did I get so lucky?" he asked.

"I'm the lucky one." Meaning that with a profundity that shook her, she leaned her head against his.

They stayed like that for a moment, before

he guided her away from the mirror and toward the door.

"My family's in the dining room," he said. "They're looking forward to meeting you."

Melanie wound her arm through his, trying not to be nervous. She wondered exactly what he'd told his dad and brothers about her, because she and Zane hadn't broached the subject yet. There'd been a lot of last-second prep for this event, a lot of time spent with Livie.

At any rate, it would be obvious to the Foleys that Melanie was more than just a nanny, and she had no idea how they might react to Zane's interest in an employee.

But when he opened the door to the dining area for her and their arms unlinked from each other, Melanie asked herself if he even *was* planning to tell them about their relationship.

What if she'd overestimated what she had with Zane?

She lifted her chin a notch and walked into the room.

The Foley men turned toward her: suave yet earthy, dignified in a way *she* only hoped to be.

Clasping her hands together in front of her, Melanie tried not to shrink into herself, even though she felt like the girl from Oklahoma again.

Had a makeover been enough?

"Melanie," Zane said, still standing close, but feeling too far, "this is my family." He gestured to his dad, a handsome man with salt-and-pepper hair and a charismatic glint in his eyes. "My father, Rex."

The patriarch came forward, extending a hand as he drawled, "Ms. Grandy, I want to thank you for all the fine work you've done. Zane tells us how Livie's come around under your care."

"Please call me Melanie. And thank you so much, Mr. Foley."

"Please, it's Rex."

As she shook hands with him, she thought about how much she liked the man's mellow tone. He had a way about him that made her feel as if she'd known him for years.

Then Zane gestured to a brother who wore a sidelong grin, and if she hadn't already been so enamored of Zane, she would've given this tall, dark charmer of a man a second glance.

"This is Jason," Zane said.

Ah, the voice on the phone, Melanie thought, recalling the day she'd overheard Zane talking about the McCords and the Santa Magdalena Diamond.

When Jason greeted her, he acted as if he were about to kiss Melanie's hand, before mischievously peering at Zane and making everyone laugh.

"Be good, you old Casanova," their father said to Jason.

Melanie laughed right along with them.

Then Zane introduced the youngest brother, who cut a lean figure dressed in the cowboy version of a suit, with a bolo tie and fancy Stetson. With his soulful eyes, Travis seemed to be the quietest of the bunch.

And as the group fell into small talk, Melanie indeed saw that he was a man of few words. Yet, he seemed the most observant, she thought, noticing that Travis had been the only one who'd really assessed her.

But—no. There was no way in the world that he could've pegged her for the imposter she felt like.

Trying harder than ever to be the new Melanie, she joined the conversation, which had turned into sibling-flavored jests about how long the brothers could last out in the heat with their full suits, and if the cooling system in the main tent would keep them from wilting.

When Livie came into the room, she was warmly greeted by her granddad and uncles, yet she gravitated to Melanie, as Zane stood close enough again for his arm to brush hers.

That was when everything brightened up.

I'm theirs, Melanie thought.

And that's all the identity she needed.

With the event in full swing, the Foleys greeted guests left and right, while the aroma of wood smoke filtered the late-afternoon air, riding the breeze that stirred the oak and willow leaves.

Interspersed among the trees, tents covered the lawn, some of them boasting games that had been set up to raise money for the hospital, some holding wine and food tastings, one bursting at the seams with a country-and-western band that had filled a temporary dance floor.

But most folks were mingling in the huge main tent, where a podium had been set up for the scheduled auction and presentations, one of which Zane would be giving. Around the floor, linen-covered tables had been set up for the coming dinner.

Currently, Zane was watching Melanie from across that tent as she and Livie chatted with a young socialite who was cradling her infant son. His daughter was clearly love-struck, and Melanie and the other woman were laughing over Livie cooing at the baby.

It felt as if half of Zane was right there with them. His family.

He found himself smiling just as they were, but little by little, it faltered. And the reason was obvious, because it'd been gnawing away at him for a while now.

He just wished he could bring himself to say those three magic words to Melanie: I. Love. You.

But every time he almost did, a creeping panic would quiet him down. "I love you" was a commitment—one he'd made to a woman before, and look how that had turned out....

"Yup," said a voice he recognized all too well as Jason's as he joined Zane, "he's a goner."

Zane glanced over, discovering that his brother was standing next to Travis and their dad—and they were all giving Zane curious, amused looks.

Travis merely drank his beer while their father reached over to grasp Zane's shoulder and give him an energetic paternal shake.

"She's a beaut, that nanny of yours," their dad said. "I'd be staring at her, too."

"When did you two start...?" Jason said, using a hand to insinuate the rest.

"That'd be none of your business." Zane took a gulp of his single-malt scotch on the rocks. He'd known this grilling would come someday, when his family saw how nuts he was about Melanie. He'd just been hoping to put it off a little longer.

But how could he, when his craving to be with her was so apparent that it practically shouted itself to all of Texas?

"Well, now," his father said. "I'm sure I speak for each of us when I say that it's just good to see you happy, Zane, whether or not you want us to know it yet."

"Damn good," Jason echoed.

Travis nodded slightly, still quiet, but Zane thought that might be because of this whole ranch mess with the McCords, which was probably weighing on his mind.

Uncomfortable with a spotlight on him, Zane made an attempt to step out of it. "Thanks, but I feel compelled to point out that I'm not the person who's grinning the most around here."

He gestured to Jason, and his brother lifted his eyebrows.

"Yeah," Zane said, relieved that he'd succeeded in getting the attention off him. "I'm talking about you."

Jason acted casual. "And why would I be grinning all that much?"

Like they didn't know.

Jason had been updating them on his plan with Penny McCord, and in private, Zane, Travis and their dad agreed that it seemed as if the guy was invested in the scheme way more than for the sake of gaining information about Travis's ranch. Forget that "the plan" hadn't yielded much of anything so far; Jason had "run into her" at a coffee house recently, and was talking about arranging yet another so-called casual encounter.

"I'd suggest," Zane said, "that there be no more wedding run-ins or random coffee dates before this thing goes too far."

"It won't," Jason said in his confident manner. "In fact—"

Without saying a word, Travis held up his hand, silencing everyone, his gaze on a trio of well-heeled people who'd just entered the tent.

"Well, I'll be damned," their father muttered when he saw them, too.

There, near the cocktail bar, were the last folks Zane had been hoping would show up.

"McCords," Jason said.

The eldest brother, Blake, walked just ahead of the rest, and when Zane spied him, he couldn't believe that there were people around the state who had the guts to compare Zane and the McCord golden child. Certainly, both were "arrogant," both were leaders of their siblings. But it was idle talk, all the same.

Behind Blake came Tate, a doctor who'd just returned from Baghdad, where he'd worked with the International Medical Corps. Although he didn't seem as easygoing as he'd once been—where was his infamous grin and the upright way he used to carry himself?— he was still escorting his girlfriend, Katerina Whitcomb-Salgar, a stunning heiress with dark hair and eyes, who filled out her dress like a movie star.

Not that Zane noticed her so much—he was zeroed in on Blake in particular.

There was a growl to Travis's voice. "What're they doing here?"

Zane answered. "Blake and Katie are both

on the hospital board of directors, and naturally Tate would come along with his girlfriend."

Across the tent, the trio stopped at the bar, where Tate seemed to distance himself from the others, staring at nothing in particular, while Blake remained at Katie's side, ordering for her, then making sure she got her drink first.

Zane's dad spoke. "Looks like Tate better pay more attention to Katie than he's doing right now. His brother seems more interested in her than *he* is."

It wasn't long before Tate's wandering gaze found the Foleys on their side of the tent.

None of them acknowledged each other, as Tate returned to Katie and Blake, where he and his brother began to talk.

Blake glanced at the Foleys, and this time Zane made a mocking toast.

The other man did the same before his

group moved a few feet from the bar, Blake turning his back on the Foleys to face Tate. When Katie left them to greet some other members of the board who were already seated at the dining tables, it wasn't Tate who tracked her with his gaze.

It was Blake.

Zane filed that away.

Soon, other partygoers blocked the McCords from view, and it was tough to see them from that point on.

"Hard to believe," Jason said, "that someone as decent as Eleanor McCord gave birth to that bunch."

As the brothers agreed, Zane noticed that his dad didn't say anything.

Actually, Zane thought that maybe there was something…odd…about the brief expression that had colored his father's gaze.

Was he remembering the young love he'd

held for Eleanor before Devon McCord ruined it?

His dad caught Zane watching him, and the older man rested a hand on Jason's arm and began guiding him out of the Foley circle.

"I believe we'll make the rounds," Rex said. "Besides, I'd like to freshen my drink."

"Have at it," Zane said, watching as his dad and Jason entered the crowd of cocktail dresses and suit jackets, the latter of which were gradually coming off as the party went on.

That left Zane and Travis alone, and his younger brother visually swept the room, not addressing Zane head-on.

"Melanie seems to be a natural with Livie," he said.

It was a real change of subject, and Zane assumed that his sibling was only bringing it up because he'd had enough of the McCords for now.

He tried to find her and Livie amongst the throng, yet failed. Maybe she'd taken his daughter outside to play some of the charity games.

"During her final interview," Zane said, "I told her she appeared too good to be true, but her records are clean—and I'd have been a fool to ignore her reference from a personal friend. And that reference was right about Melanie. She really is an outstanding…" he tripped over the word "…nanny."

Travis sent Zane a long, hard look.

"What?" Zane asked.

"Nothing." Travis shook his head and drank his beer.

Then he excused himself, saying that he saw an old friend and wanted to say hello.

As Travis left, Zane kept an eye on his brother, wondering what the hell his comments had been about. Travis's reticence even burned him a little, because this was Melanie—the best woman Zane had ever...

Loved?

God, why did that notion rattle him every time?

But he knew: Danielle. History repeating.

He should've been over it, but he wasn't.

Zane finished his drink, and was just about to leave his spot, when Livie jumped in front of him, all smiles and snow-cone blue around her mouth.

No matter what kind of mood he might've been in, he laughed, and Melanie showed up with a facial wipe, as if she'd been chasing Livie around with it.

"Come here, you," she said to the girl.

Exasperated, Livie closed her eyes and raised her face so Melanie could clean her up. Meanwhile, in diamonds and silk, Melanie grinned at Zane.

Her love for Livie—and for him?—shone through, and he wanted to kiss her, right here, right now. Wanted to thread his fingers through her blond hair and bring her close, tasting her, consuming her.

"This party is going off well," she said when she was done with Livie.

The girl spotted another child her age close by and shyly wandered over while both he and Melanie began to follow, their steps slow, unhurried.

"Thanks to you and the staff, the event's going to haul in more than ever," he said, meaning it as a compliment.

But when her cheeks went pink, he realized that she'd paid more attention to being lumped together with the other employees than in what he'd actually been saying.

"Hey, now." He halted them both near Livie at the side of the tent, where she'd sat down on the grass near the other girl, who introduced herself to Livie by showing her a doll she was playing with.

Zane touched Melanie's arm, fingertips on skin, sending voltage through her. "You know what I meant."

"Yes," she said, smiling, even though he could tell it was forced. "I know."

All the voices around them seemed to drop off into nothing as Zane looked into her eyes, the blue capturing him.

His future. His Melanie.

Not caring who saw, he slipped his hand to the small of her back, where her dress dipped.

Her flesh, silky warmth.

"You're tempting me to take you right out of here," he said softly.

Her smile went dreamy, and it perked up his heartbeat.

They kept walking until they heard a

familiar chuckle, and Zane almost took his hand away from her.

But he didn't.

Instead, he kept it right where it was, claiming Melanie, for anyone to see.

Jason was still laughing as Zane and Melanie halted near his brother and his father. The other two seemed to be sharing some kind of private joke.

When their dad saw Zane, he assumed a "you're not going to believe this" glance, including them in the conversation. "Odd what you hear during a party when people think their conversation's being covered by all the chatter around them."

Zane got a bad feeling about this.

"If you're thinking," Jason said to Zane, "that we sidled right up to the bar, unseen by Blake and Tate, you'd be right."

Their father had the grace to look sheepish.

"We only overheard them for a short while, and not on purpose…at first."

"I hope they didn't see you," Zane said.

"No. The McCord boys went off to join Katie before they even looked our way."

Clearly, Jason had only been continuing his information-culling "plan," and with the possibility of some progress in that area, Zane's fingers tightened on Melanie's back.

It made him talk before he really thought about what he was saying.

"If you don't mind," he whispered, leaning toward her so only she would hear, "this is business. I'll find you in a bit."

Her spine straightened, and he caught a pained cloud in her gaze as she murmured something about Livie, then left before he realized what had just truly happened.

Business. He'd dismissed her because of it, and she knew it.

Was she wondering if she came in second to office hours and the McCords?

Surely she realized how he truly felt about her—even if he hadn't told her in so many words....

Jason continued, totally unaware of Zane's muddled emotions.

"If we had any doubts about money troubles in the McCord camp," his brother said, "we shouldn't anymore."

"Blake McCord didn't say anything outright," their father added. "He's damned proud, and he seemed reluctant to even be talking about it to Tate."

Zane watched from afar as Melanie stood next to Livie while his daughter played with the other little girl.

He wanted to be there.

But he had to see to the McCords, too. Business was...more important than anything?

"Zane?" Jason asked.

He glanced back at his brother and dad, who were gauging him as if he'd dropped his brain somewhere on the floor and hadn't ever picked it back up.

"I'm listening," he said, but he sounded as distracted as he felt.

As his father kept measuring up Zane, Jason went ahead.

"We couldn't hear very well, only a phrase here and there, but Blake and Tate mentioned the Santa Magdalena Diamond, all right. Something about how it relates to Travis's ranch and the land deed that Grandpa Gavin lost to Harry McCord in that poker game. So, as you can tell, Zane, my instincts were right. Never doubt a man with a plan."

Zane didn't even have time to chuff before his dad added, "It sounds like there're some clues on that deed that lead to one of the property's abandoned mines."

"The Eagle," Jason said, referring to the name given to just one of the five mines. "But, again, that's all we could hear, so I don't know how they got from point A to B and so on." He grinned that lady-killer grin. "I'll find out, though."

With Penny McCord, Zane thought.

Jason was, by now, scanning the crowd in his charming, cocky way, as if it was time to move on, meet some women, go from there. "Blake mentioned their sister Paige's name along with the words *'diamond'* and *'mine'*, and I figure, since she and Penny are twins, they've got to be close. Penny's going to know something about whatever scheme Paige is cooking up along with her brothers."

"Good, Jace," Zane said. "That sounds reasonable."

But once again he was looking away from the conversation, just like his brother, and it had nothing to do with anyone but Melanie. Yet, she and Livie weren't in the same place anymore.

They were gone.

A pang got to him, but it wasn't just because he already missed her.

When he caught up to her, how was he going to explain his attachment to business at her and Livie's expense?

As he tried to figure it all out, the party went on around him, even though, without her nearby, it was so much less festive.

Chapter Eleven

The party was over, and as the crews deconstructed the tents and tidied up, Zane knew he needed to do a bit of the same with Melanie.

Take apart the hurt he'd seen after he'd dismissed her. Clean up the mess he'd left.

He didn't find her again until he got back to the house. She was putting Livie to bed, and he joined in what had become a nightly ritual, with his daughter asking him to read from one of those vividly illustrated Golden Books.

Then, in turn, he and Melanie kissed Livie good-night.

They would seem like a real family to anyone who casually looked in on them, Zane thought. But he sure hadn't treated Melanie like a true part of his life tonight.

She told him that she was going to get ready for bed in her room, then come to his, as she'd been doing for a while now, in order to keep from flaunting their sleeping arrangements. So he went to his own quarters, took a shower and put on his sweatpants and T-shirt. Then he waited for her, tempted by a pile of contracts near the bed, but denying the call of work.

Because that had been the issue, he thought. Work. The McCords.

And right now, neither of them appealed.

When Melanie took a longer time in coming than he'd anticipated, he couldn't wait any longer, so he headed for her room and knocked on the door.

"Come in," she said, sounding far away.

But he was here to make sure she would always be close.

The realization washed through him. He needed to let her know, once and for all, exactly how much he'd come to love her, how much she added to his and Livie's lives.

And he was ready, by God. So ready to lay himself out there because, out of everyone in this world, he could trust Melanie. She had already accepted everything about him, and it was up to Zane to let her know that he was going to do the same with her.

Nerves humming, he found her dressed in a white peignoir, taking off her makeup. The outfit was one he'd recently bought, lacy, silken, as refined as she was becoming more and more each day. Her hair was down around her shoulders, combed out, soft.

Zane loved to see the changes in her, but he would always value the image of the woman in the knockoff-quality business suit, too.

Leaning against the bathroom door frame, he said, "Long time, no see."

She gestured toward her half-removed makeup; she'd worn more than usual for the party. "I've got a lot more to deal with tonight."

He took a deep breath, ready to apologize for how he'd treated her. "Tell me about it."

At first, he wasn't sure why her shoulders slumped a little. But then he realized she had taken his own comment to mean that he'd been forced to deal with the extra burden of the McCords during the party.

Was she reliving that moment he told her that he needed to take care of business? That thoughtless instant when he'd basically let her know that she was secondary to his other pursuits?

Well, he was going to put that worry to rest. He was a new man because of her, and second by second, everything that used to consume him became more irrelevant.

She finished taking off her makeup.

"Melanie," he said, allowing her name to carry all the affection and adoration he felt.

She turned away from the mirror, and he noticed how beautiful she still was, with or without those cosmetics.

"Tonight," he said, "I made the mistake of putting you off because of business. It was wrong, and I want you to know that I'm never going to do it again."

She smiled softly, but there was a tinge of sadness to the gesture, too, and he wondered if there was a lot more to tonight than he was realizing.

Even so, he was going to finish the apology. Then they could move on.

"I don't want there to be any secrets between us," he added. "I want to be able to come home at night at a decent hour, be with you and Livie, then talk to you about anything, whether it's about what I'm doing at the office or it's about the McCords." He grasped one of her hands. "I want to be as open with you as you've been with me."

She lowered her gaze, but he thought he saw the blue of her eyes go cloudy with something he couldn't begin to fathom.

So he touched on everything she should know as the woman he wanted to spend the rest of his life with: a brief version of history between the Foleys and McCords, the Santa Magdalena Diamond, this whole issue with Jason's plan and how it affected the way Zane had acted with her at the event today.

She listened, seeming to grow more uncomfortable with every passing minute, until, at the end, he said, "You look like you don't want to hear any of this."

It was as if she was trying to make some kind of heavy decision, and she held his hand to her chest, cradling it.

Then she sighed, releasing him before she walked out of the bathroom.

"I do want to hear all of it," she finally said as she sat on a chair near the bed, her hands folded in her lap, her knuckles going white with the pressure she was putting on them. "I...I *did* hear, Zane."

What the hell did she mean?

She continued, watching him as if she meant to test him with what she was about to say. "During our second interview, I forgot my suit jacket in your study, and I went back to get it. But you were on the phone with Jason. I loitered in the hallway and heard what you two were talking about, so I already knew about the diamond and Jason's plans with Penny McCord."

"You were eavesdropping on me?"

She nodded, still measuring him with that cautious gaze. Again, he thought there might be more to this than the obvious.

"I started listening in," she said, "because Jason asked you about me, and I was curious, because even early on I was smitten with you."

Zane didn't know whether to be angry or touched. Both emotions warred with each other, and much to his surprise, touched was winning.

"So," he said, "this whole time you knew about that piece of business."

"I was embarrassed to tell you."

He hated that she felt this way, hated that she looked so sad. And even though he wished she'd told him about this earlier, she didn't need to be punished any further.

But it was funny, he thought, because, only weeks ago he would've been quick to strike out with a lot more defensive ire.

"What else haven't you told me yet?" he asked, almost in jest.

Yet, she must have misconstrued his tone, because her face paled.

A tiny niggle—a guarded habit he thought he had overcome—lashed at him.

What's she hiding? How's this woman going to hurt you, and are you just going to stand there letting her do it?

But he was overreacting. And he didn't want to disappoint her like that. God, he wanted to make her the happiest woman on earth, and if she had believed that she couldn't confide in him, he bore that responsibility.

He took a seat on the bed. "What do you say we come clean with each other right now. About anything and everything."

She closed her eyes, biting her lip so hard that he thought it might start bleeding.

In spite of not understanding what this was about, he saw her slipping away from him with every moment that she couldn't meet his gaze.

And he couldn't take it.

He couldn't lose Melanie.

"I'll start," he told her. "I made a big mistake today. A couple of them, actually. The first one was in not making it crystal clear to everyone at that party that you and I are together. I should have, even though all they had to do was look at me to see that I'm yours."

She shook her head. "Zane, that's not—"

But he couldn't be stopped. *She* was what he wanted. *She* was what he was stepping up and claiming right damned now.

"My second mistake," he said, "was excluding you from a part of my life that I haven't been able to let go of. Maybe I thought that my job—my old existence—was going to be my safety net, just in case you and I didn't work out. But I'm not going to do that anymore."

Her eyes were getting a sheen to them, but it didn't look like the start of happy crying. It looked like frustration.

"If you say it won't happen again," she said, her voice wobbling, "it won't. But it's been a long day. Maybe we should sleep on this, and…"

He leaned forward to cup her jaw with one hand. "Melanie, I've been so afraid of failing as a husband. As a father. But by protecting myself, I've been setting us up for failure all along."

"No…" She stared at her lap, where her hands were still clenched. Then, as a single tear spilled down her cheek, she fended off a sob. "It hasn't just been you, Zane. I've done things to set us up, too."

Right. Zane almost laughed, because the opposite was true.

He stroked her hair back from her face, wishing that she would look at him again, that he could see the steadiness in her gaze that he'd come to treasure.

He loved this woman, and by not telling her before tonight, he had been giving her up slowly but surely.

So he got to his knee at the foot of her chair, holding her hand in the two of his.

"I love you, Melanie."

A tiny sound came from her throat—another sob?

But why?

He kept on. "I want you with me, now and always, and I can't imagine a future without you in it." He rested his forehead against their hands, feverish, carried away. "Marry me. Be with me. Spend the rest of your life with me."

Pressing his lips to her fingers, he waited for her answer.

Yet, tears seemed to be her only response.

Even as joy welled within Melanie, it was blocked by the unrestrained fear of the look she would see in Zane's eyes when she told him who she was and where she'd come from.

He would be disgusted, she thought. And although he hadn't reacted as badly as she'd believed he would when she tested him with her minisecret about eavesdropping on him and Jason, she was sure that wouldn't hold true with her bigger bombshell.

Nevertheless, she'd come close to revealing her history when Zane had said that he didn't want there to be anything between them.

So close.

Yet, then she'd come to her senses, because how could one of the world's biggest tycoons have any kind of positive reaction to her mortifying past?

How could a man who hadn't been big on trust in the first place ever forgive her?

She actually wasn't afraid of him getting angry, either; in fact, she would welcome it because it would be well deserved. It was his disappointment that would get her.

He would be disappointed that, even after they'd made love and grown closer every day, she'd backed away from being truthful with him. And he would be disappointed that she wasn't the woman he'd fallen for.

As the seconds dragged by, Zane raised his gaze, still clasping her hand while retaining the fervid glow that had come along with his proposal.

She held to him tighter, not wanting to let go.

But the longer she didn't give him an answer, the more the shadows began to crawl back into his eyes.

And those shadows were encroaching because of *her,* not Danielle.

He released her hand, and she realized that he'd already taken her hesitation for a refusal.

Tears rolled down her face now, and she felt as if a fist had a grip inside her chest.

"For some reason," he said, staying on his knee, "I thought a proposal would turn out differently. I pictured you crying from happiness, not…this."

Melanie opened her mouth to say something to make him feel better, but the words balled in her throat, and she feared she would choke on them.

She just wanted to tell him that she hadn't

refused him in the least. That he was the best thing that had ever happened to her and all she wanted to do was make sure they stayed in love.

But how could they do that when the only way to appease him was to be truthful? She wouldn't pile more lies on top of the ones she'd already committed.

He got to his feet. "I guess I just bring out the tears in women."

She shook her head, but it was like the sky was crashing down on her, and she knew that she couldn't let this continue any longer.

"Zane," she said, barreling ahead. "I'm crying because—"

He held up a hand, halting every word she didn't want to say.

The proud man she'd met during those first interviews was back, his posture stiff, his tone stern, his gaze dark and guarded. But underneath it all, she could see that he was crushed, and she had done that to Zane.

Her—the woman who'd had such good intentions with Livie, with him….

He headed for the door. "I'm leaving. You just stay here with Livie."

She bolted to her feet, her heart ripping out of her chest, but as he opened the door, his gaze was so full of wounded rage that it stopped Melanie in her tracks.

"Don't come after me, understand?" he said. "I…"

His voice caught and he went out the door, shutting it softly behind him, leaving her frozen in guilt and devastation.

Her crying was the only sound she heard. She'd been so afraid of seeing disgust, but there was no way his reaction to her past could've been any worse than this. No way she could have done any more damage to him and, by extension, Livie.

At the idea of his daughter returning to the shadow she'd also been, Melanie forced herself to move, to open the door, then go toward his room. She had to tell him everything so that he would know she'd wanted to say yes.

Yes and yes, a million times over.

But when she got to his room it was empty.

And after she went to his window to see if she could catch sight of any taillights streaking away from the main house, she went back to her room for her cell phone and tried Zane's number.

As his voice mail intercepted her call, she began to understand just what "empty" really meant.

Zane only made it to the massive on-property garage, where he was about to take off in one of the cars—he barely even knew which one—before he asked himself just where he was going.

To Dallas, so he could fade into his townhouse?

To the office, so he could go back to a place that didn't hold as much attraction for him now?

He had no idea where he should go, but he did know that he'd put his heart on the line and Melanie hadn't taken it.

Anguish made him lean against a car door. All those feelings he'd suppressed for years were clawing him apart.

No wonder he'd banished them.

But Melanie—God, he couldn't even think of her name without another claw swiping at him… She had to be just as in love with him as he was with her. He'd been sure of it. And he knew she would walk through fire for Livie, too.

So what had gone wrong?

He replayed everything in his mind: their talk, her reactions…

And he realized now that she'd been close to crying even before he'd gotten to the proposal.

"It hasn't just been you, Zane," she had said. "I've done things to set us up, too."

And in his eagerness to make up for all he'd done wrong today, he'd completely ignored whatever she'd been working up to telling him.

What *had* she been attempting to say before he'd rushed into the proposal?

And what if everything hinged on the answer?

But even as he wondered, he left the car and made his way out of the garage, still not sure where he was off to. Still not sure if he had the courage to let himself feel again, to get back what he'd given up after Danielle's death.

As he walked, getting his head together, he stayed within view of the mansion, where

Melanie might still be waiting for him if he found it within himself to go back inside.

Unfeeling, Melanie had gone from Zane's room back to her own.

Although she held the attacking emotions at bay, they still raced around in a swirl of despair and confusion: should she go to the garage to see if Zane had taken a car out? And how would she even know if he had?

Instead, she walked through the house, hoping to find him in a sitting or dining room. Yet he wasn't anywhere around, and the questions increased in volume, nearly deafening her.

When Melanie arrived back at her room, the buzz of her mind came to a screeching halt as she found Livie at her door.

She was wearing a pair of new summer pajamas Zane had purchased for her, and they were decorated with R2-D2s, replacing the old pajamas Livie had used to make that Father's Day tie.

At the reminder of better times, Melanie got to her knees and pulled Livie into an embrace, burying her face in the girl's hair and holding back the threat of more tears.

Livie hugged her, too, patting her nanny's back. She was sleepy, and right now Melanie could get away with a short hug before the girl caught on that something was wrong.

Get it together, Melanie thought. *Don't let Livie see how upset you are. Don't pile this on her.*

So she held back her sorrow, attempting to dry her tears before Livie saw them.

She put on the perfect nanny smile for the child, trying to fool both of them. "I thought you'd be sleeping straight through the night."

Melanie's voice was thick, and she told herself to try harder.

Livie rubbed her eyes. "I thought I heard daddy in the halls and I couldn't sleep again. Why isn't he in his room?"

"He's somewhere around," Melanie said. "But I'm sure he's going to be back in his room soon."

If anything, Melanie would go after Zane herself, returning him here for Livie's sake. She would understand if he didn't want anything more to do with *her,* but she would still keep battling for this little girl.

And as Melanie put her hands on the child's arms, she realized that she'd come so close to having Livie be *her* little girl, too. Yet she'd allowed ugly pride to get in the way.

Pride and self-preservation, she thought. She'd been practicing it just as much as Zane had.

"Ms. Grandy?" Livie asked, tilting her head.

"What is it, sweetheart?"

The child's eyes were as serious as they'd been the day they met, and Melanie couldn't bear to see her return to the shadows, just like her father.

"Someday," the girl said, "are *you* going to not be in your room?"

Melanie tried not to jerk away from the question. She had seen it in Livie's eyes often, and she'd only been waiting for the child to ask it, so Melanie had merely done her best to always let the girl know that her nanny would be around, no matter what.

And this was the "no matter what," wasn't it?

Yet, what if Zane did fire her? How could she reassure Livie without giving her false promises?

"I'll always be a part of your life, Livie," she said.

And she meant it, even if she had to call or write long, long letters or...

"Oh," the little girl said, revealing that Melanie's answer wasn't the one she wanted.

But Melanie couldn't lie, not above what she'd already done to Zane.

As the child lowered her head, Melanie picked her up, cradling her small body, and started off for the girl's room.

"I'll be wherever you need me," she whispered to the child, who wrapped her arms around Melanie. "And I mean that. Never forget it, Livie."

As she lay her charge down to sleep again, shutting out the lights after Livie finally blanked out, Melanie went back to her room, preparing herself for a long, lonely night. She was going to stay here in case Livie woke up again, but come morning, she would hunt Zane down if she had to.

Hours passed, the dark outlines of the trees outside shifting over the walls. But, near dawn, just when Melanie was half asleep, her burning eyes no longer able to stay open, she thought she heard footsteps creaking up the stairway.

She sat up in bed, hoping.

Praying it was Zane.

Chapter Twelve

Zane took the stairs, his gaze fixed at the very top of them.

For most of the night he'd sorted things out on the lawn, which had become empty, once the tents were taken down and the laughter from less than a day ago had died.

Melanie's laughter, Melanie's smiles.

He'd sat on that lawn, debating with himself until he ultimately decided that he wasn't going to accept things as they'd ended tonight.

He was going to go back into that mansion and put himself out there again, no matter how much of a wreck it might make him in the end. He owed Livie that much.

And he owed himself.

When he reached the top of the steps and came to Melanie's door, he didn't even knock. He just opened it, his blood jerking as the predawn room revealed her sitting up in bed, as if she'd heard him coming up the stairs.

As the air went still around them, chopped into sections by his heartbeat, they sat there, watching each other. His body rhythms went off the charts, merely because he was near her—the woman he couldn't stop loving, even if she hadn't accepted his offer of marriage.

He could hear her breathing, see her chest moving underneath the nightdress he'd so carefully chosen for her, knowing how she'd look in…and out…of it.

"I…" She put a hand to her heart, as if to stop it from punching its way out of her. "I thought you might have left Tall Oaks for good."

Did she think he was still the man who continually distanced himself from life?

It stung to believe that she thought he hadn't changed at all.

"I was on the property the entire time," he said. "I wasn't about to go anywhere without hearing why you turned me down."

"I never said no, Zane—"

"Melanie, I know damned well when you refuse something, whether it's a gift or a proposal."

Her hand fell away from her chest in response to the whiplash tone he'd used; but he was hurt, too. He wouldn't admit it: his ego, his intentions…his very soul. Bruised and aching.

When she spoke her voice shook, and he took a step toward her before halting, fisting his hands with the effort. He couldn't lay himself bare to her again—not without a sign from her.

"I never wanted you to know," she said, lowering her head, her blond hair covering most of her face so he couldn't see it, not even by the faint light in the room. "But I realized that I'd have to tell you someday, even though I kept procrastinating...*hoping* I could somehow outrun myself. And, tonight, *I* was the only thing holding myself back. All I wanted to do was jump up and accept your proposal, Zane. I would've said yes in a heartbeat, if I could have."

She was coming around to what she meant when she said that she was "setting them up," and he just wanted her to get there.

"And why can't you say yes?" he asked. "What's going on, Melanie?"

She brought her knees up, wrapping her arms around them. It was a shelter he recognized all too well, because he'd felt like that inside for a long time.

"I'm ashamed to tell you," she whispered raggedly. "I always have been."

A tug of war pulled him toward her and away from her at the same time.

Yet, all he could do was wait for her, because he wasn't going to leave this room without the truth.

"Ashamed of what?" he prompted.

"Ashamed of…me." She bit her lip, as if trying to keep herself from crying again, but her voice went shaky and thick anyway. "Of who I really am."

Of who she…?

His mind blanked for a minute, but then it started to piece together what was what.

"Today's party…" he began. "It was the first time you were in my world, and you felt out of place as the family nanny. That's why you think I didn't want to claim you in front of God and country—because you believe we were all thinking that a girl like you didn't belong."

She started to glance up, and he took a step closer to the bed.

"You're wrong, Melanie," he added. "Maybe I'm slow to announce a relationship after what happened with my first marriage, but that has nothing to do with you."

Her next words froze him.

"That's not it at all, Zane. I've been lying to you."

And there it was—stark and simple, enough to make him take a step back. His vision swirled as his mind struggled to catch up.

Had he made the day's biggest mistake in coming up here again?

"Lying…how?" he asked.

"There're some details," she said quietly,

the shame weighing on her tone, "that I left off my resume."

The oxygen deserted him, but he still managed to ask, "Then who *are* you?"

She paused, then looked him straight in the eyes. He could tell it was taking every bit of strength she had to do it.

"I'm a girl who was raised dirt-poor. A woman who took up dancing in a Vegas casino to make ends meet for her family back in Oklahoma. A person you would've never hired if you'd known."

His first urge was to be angry with her for lying to him—right now he couldn't give less of a crap about her being poor or dancing. But Danielle had hidden things from him, and he'd promised that it would never happen again. Yet here he was, and...

And his heart was breaking as Melanie lowered her head again, shaking it in such obvious self-hatred that he couldn't take it.

He saw what he'd been like only weeks ago, before she'd come along. He would have fired her after this revelation. Banished her from his life.

But, calling on what she had taught him about loving and patience, he came to sit on the bed near her, resting a hand on her sheet-covered ankle. That seemed to steady her a bit.

She angrily wiped the tears from her eyes. "Why aren't you throwing me out yet?"

Zane kept holding on. "Just explain this to me."

Melanie didn't speak for a moment. But then, tentatively, she told him everything; as she went along, her words came faster and faster, and she was relieved to be rid of them.

She talked of her mother's tendency to date the wrong men, how Melanie didn't even know the identity of her own father, how her mom had a constant need for loans and how that had led to dancing in the Grand Illusion casino.

Then she told him of her decision to wipe that part of her life off the map and head for greener pastures.

Every confession was a slice to Melanie's hopes, as she watched his expression, which hadn't changed since he'd sat on the bed.

But she'd known it would turn out this way. And she wouldn't love Zane any less for cutting her loose when she was done speaking.

"I only hoped to become the person I always believed I could be," she finally said, struggling to keep from breaking apart. "And I know I might not have gone about it in the best ways possible, but I think I did some good for me, and for others. At least, I wanted to."

"You did a lot of good."

Melanie's spirits rose, but then crashed again as she searched his face for any meaning beyond what he'd just said. Yet, he was still inscrutable, and she feared he'd go back to being halfway across the world from her, even though he was sitting right there.

That's what hurt the most about this, she realized. The fact that she'd put him in a position where he was disappointed in someone once more.

He took his hand off her ankle, and it felt as if she were alone—just as utterly and truly alone as she had known her life's story would make her if anyone discovered it.

"I wish you would've just told me," Zane said.

"When? I wanted the nanny job. I adored Livie from the first time I met her, and I knew that you'd never hire a downtrodden ex-showgirl to raise your child."

He started to protest but didn't make it all the way through.

"I didn't know you then," he said instead. "So you're right—no matter how quickly I needed to hire someone, I probably wouldn't have chosen you."

"And if you hadn't hired me," she added, "we would've never…"

She couldn't say it. It seemed like such an impossibility right now—something that had slipped right through her fingers.

But he finished for her. "We would've never fallen in love."

Just the sound of it drilled into her, and she forced herself not to lose her emotional hold again.

"I wouldn't blame you if you never forgave me," she said. "I'd deserve that, because by not telling you about myself, I kept buying stolen time. I had a beautiful daughter in

Livie. I had a family I would've done any-thing for." She swallowed, and it felt as if a rock was being wedged down her throat. "And I had you. So I don't regret what I did, Zane, even if it's only because it gave me all of that, until I couldn't have it anymore."

He stood, and panic flared through her.

He's really leaving this time, she thought. *And I can't do anything about it.*

She bolted to her knees anyway, willing to do anything for him, just as she'd said.

But then he paused, robbing her of speech as she sucked in a hopeful breath.

"I've spent a lot of time unable to forgive," he said, his words mangled.

Forgive?

She wondered if he would have it within himself to forgive her, and the hope grew until it pierced her chest from the inside out.

"There were years," he continued, "where I

blamed fate for bringing the worst down on me with Danielle. And those years were such a damned waste." He leaned toward her. "Back then, I would've been angrier than hell with you, Melanie. But…"

Before she knew what was happening, he scooped her against him, crushing his mouth to hers in a kiss so raw that she crumbled beneath him.

He hadn't left.

He wasn't going anywhere.

As his mouth ravished hers, she took his head between her palms, keeping a hold of him, taking everything he was offering, because *he* was all she needed.

No diamonds, no cars—he was the greatest gift of all.

He swept his tongue into her mouth, and she met it with her own, the kiss wet and greedy, wild with the passion she would never lose for him.

A forever love, she thought. She'd never hoped to find one, but here it was, with Zane.

He suspended the kiss while easing her backward into the crook of his arm.

"I can't be angry with you," he said. "I found you, and I'm not letting you go that easily."

Pure bliss shot through her, sizzling every cell and making her laugh on a sob—but now it was one of joy, not sadness, and he seemed to realize that.

"Is that a yes?" he asked, his tone rough, like a man on the edge.

This time she answered right away.

"Yes," she said. "Yes, yes, yes."

And she kept saying it, even while his mouth descended on hers again and he lowered her to the bed. He kept kissing her to within an inch of consciousness, as her world reeled, creating something out of what she thought to have been nothing.

As he lifted his head from hers just to look into her eyes, the morning came through the window and turned over in one instant of awakening sunlight.

"Yes," he repeated, as if rolling the word over them both.

It felt as if she were on a mountaintop, the wind whipping around her, the air thin in her lungs. "What will we tell your family?"

"That we're getting married as soon as possible."

Nerves mingled with her light-headedness, and he noticed her anxiety about how the Foleys—and everyone else—might react to him marrying his nanny.

"Don't worry," he said, tracing his fingertips over her collarbone. "They like you. Believe me, they won't be thinking I've married someone who…"

He trailed off.

"Is so different from you?" she finished, saving him from having to finish.

His eyes took on a warrior's glint—the brash, arrogant gleam that had defined him in business. But now she was what he clearly intended to fight for.

"If you don't want to tell them about your personal details," he said, "you don't have to. It's none of anyone's business but our own."

"And the press?"

"I know how to manage the press. But if it comes down to it, I'll talk for days about the woman who pulled herself up by the boot-straps and made herself into the force who changed my life."

Melanie touched his face. "You would do that?"

"Hey, didn't Cinderella come from the ashes before she started wearing ball gowns?"

Oh, he knew just how to put it.

"Besides," he continued, "I fell in love with a woman who doesn't even need ball gowns to shine."

Melting. She couldn't stop melting.

But he must've seen the remaining fear that mingled with her excitement.

"Maybe," he said, "we could take it a little slower then? Would it help if we eased you into my lifestyle?"

"Zane, you wouldn't mind?"

"No, Melanie."

She could tell that he wasn't taking this as another hesitation on her part, but just to emphasize how much she loved him, she pulled him down to her, tenderly fitting her lips to his.

And when she had kissed him, she said, "So, I assume we'll be keeping our engagement quiet for the time being, except with Livie? I can't imagine not telling her."

Melanie would bet her life that his—no *their*—daughter wouldn't say a word. She had all the trust in existence for Livie.

"Then we'll tell her." Zane ran a hand through Melanie's hair as a changing light filtered through his gaze.

He smiled. "So…a dancing girl, huh?"

She nodded, ready for the shame to cover her again, but when she saw Zane's heart in his eyes, too, the mortification never came.

"I guess," he added, "during our long engagement, I'll just have to make sure you see yourself as I do, then you'll be calling every newspaper in the nation with the announcement."

She had no doubt that in no time at all she would. His love had that much power.

"I love you, Zane."

"And I love you. I just wish the whole world could know about it sooner. But I'd do anything for you, Melanie." He pressed his lips to hers. "Anything."

As she responded to him with a desire that matched his own, Zane reveled in the knowledge that every bit of Melanie was his: her future, her present and now even her past, which she'd finally released, just as he'd let go of his, too.

And in giving it up, he'd found something he'd never expected—a heart.

Melanie had been the one to help him rediscover it, he knew, and that mattered more to him than any of her history.

Still kissing her, he dragged her lacy nightie off her shoulders, then down the rest of her body, exposing every inch of her to the emerging blush of sunrise. When she was naked, he went back on his haunches, just to get his fill of her.

Then again, he knew he'd never be able to, and that was because she was about more than just a slender, streamlined body. More than long legs and perfect breasts. She was his soul, regenerating him moment by moment.

Blood pounded through him, heating him up, making him feel more alive than ever, as he parted her legs and bent to her.

He touched his mouth to the soft area between her thighs, and she moaned, encouraging him. Then he ran his tongue through her folds, up, then up again, until she was arching away from the mattress and fisting his hair.

"A long, very slow engagement," she said on a laugh that sounded so cleansed that he couldn't help but to feel the same way.

"And more," he said before separating her and loving her thoroughly, making her churn her hips, rocking against him as he kept kissing, kept bringing her to the brink…

…and beyond.

After she climaxed, he stripped off his shirt, then the sweatpants he was straining against.

He fit himself over her body, feeling her sleek muscles against his own, as his erection nudged her.

"Do we…?" she began to ask on a breath.

He knew she was asking about a condom.

"I don't want anything to come between us," he said, repeating what he'd told her earlier.

Melanie cupped his face, her expression glowing with the love she'd confessed, along with everything else.

"Me, either," she said. "I want it *all* with you, Zane."

Then, so slowly that it slayed him, she

skimmed her fingers down his chest, his stomach, resting them on his length, which was pulsing in anticipation of being inside her.

She made his wish come true, guiding him into her and then rising up to take him all the way in.

At first, his vision went blank at the feel of her, but it returned in blazing color as he slid out, then in, again and again, as she kept time with him.

Wanting to go deeper, wanting everything he could get from her, he lifted one of her legs, and she answered by bending it to the side.

Her flexibility pumped him, and he drove into her once more…twice more…another time….

Pressure curled inside of him, melting inward, then arching. Arching some more.

And his passion kept arching, escalating, expanding into something like a bridge stretching from him to her, connecting them, its apex climbing and climbing until…

The arch shattered, but the link remained, as he kept hold of Melanie, his future wife, the woman he would forgive just about anything.

Because love had allowed it, he thought. Love made anything possible.

He stayed inside her as they leisurely kissed, his arm curled over her head, one of her legs wrapped around him.

It wasn't until long afterward, when the sun had risen all the way and they'd showered together, that they got ready to tell Livie the toughest secret she would ever have to keep.

At least until Zane could show Melanie that the world didn't matter when it came to them.

"Do you think Livie will be…happy?" Melanie asked while donning a sundress.

"I can't believe you'd think otherwise." He took her into his arms. "My daughter loves you beyond comprehension, just like I do."

Her smile was filled with wonder, as if she couldn't believe love was this simple. He could hardly believe it either, but they were going to make it so.

He'd forgiven her, and it'd been easy.

Still, a stray notion chewed at the back of his mind.

Forgiveness. If Melanie had taught him so much that he could forgive *her,* shouldn't he let it branch out to other parts of his life?

The image of the Santa Magdalena Diamond floated through his consciousness, but he blanked it out.

He wasn't going to think of the McCords now.

He wasn't going to think about them for a good, long while.

Taking Melanie's hand, he led her out of the

room and to Livie's. And when they awakened her, she smiled up at them, as if unsurprised to see them together, greeting her first thing in the morning.

Zane squeezed Melanie's hand, then asked his daughter, "Can you keep a secret?"

Livie blinked, nodding eagerly as she made her way to a sitting position.

Melanie beamed. "When I told you I'm never going anywhere, I meant it."

As the child's eyes grew wider, Zane and Melanie explained the rest, and when they were done, she bounded into their arms, hugging them with a fierceness that told him she'd been hoping for this moment.

And when they broke apart to laugh with each other, as the girl started firing off when, where, why and how questions, Zane didn't see his past in his daughter anymore.

He just saw Livie—a happy little girl who wanted to move forward, too.

Soon, they were all embracing again, the family they were meant to be.

* * * * *